THE DRAGONS OF CAMELON

by

Kim Kacoroski

This book is a work of fiction. Names, characters, places, and incidents are either the product of the author's imagination or are used fictitiously. Any resemblance to actual persons, living or dead, or to actual events or locales is entirely coincidental.

Cover art illustrations by Kim Kacoroski, Phillipe Velasquez, and Masha Tatarintsev

Visit the author website:
http://kimkacoroski.com

ISBN: 978-1-947036-05-5 (Paperback)

Version 2017.21.03

Book Two of Camelon Series

The Dragons of Camelon II

Other Books in the Camelon Series

The Promise of Camelon I

History of the World According to the Druids III

New Beginnings IV

The Kingdom of the Golden Tara V

Bridges of Flight before the American Revolution VI

Books in the Oblivion Series

Escape from Oblivion I

Beyond Oblivion II

Oblivion's Edge III

Oblivion's Deal IV

Flight from Oblivion V

Books in the Flight Series

Flight from Oblivion I

Eagle's Flight in the American Revolution II

Flight of the Ascendants in the American Revolution III

Choices from the American Revolution IV

Bridges of Flight before the American Revolution V

Testimony VI

INTRODUCTION

Tune References in **THE DRAGONS OF CAMELON** *convey the gravity of salvaging a civilization on the wings of inspiration. Contemporary writings of the historical period romanticize the Turks's invasion, which fails to represent the efforts of the survivors. Songs of the present capture the devastation wrought by the power grabs of the various factions of the dying Roman Empire. Few people today distinguish the natives from the conquerors. Setting their story to music gives the reader some idea of the gravity of the situation that the natives willingly confronted.*

Chapter One

If you don't like it

Spit it out

If you want to say something

Spit it out

Without vanity or ambivalence

Tune Reference: *December*

----Collective Soul

ON A DARK and snowy morning. Joslin peered past the coast of present-day Wales and saw her friends, the Sea Dragons. The phosphorescence from the sea reflected on their shiny, shimmering scales. They were elegant, beautiful, grand creatures that gracefully swirled and flitted through the frothy waves. Her father had taught her how to contact them as a very small child. Being eight years old, she had easily mastered the ability to communicate with Sea Dragons.

Today she needed their help. Being the most magnificent, benevolent creatures that she knew, she wanted to hear what they had to say on the matter. Joslin trusted no one else. Both her parents, Arcas and Laticia, had died some time ago, and no one except the Sea Dragons understood her world.

"Hello there, young Joslin!" Earl, the brilliant garnet sea dragon, communicated wordlessly. "What brings you to the sea on this frigid, December morning?"

"I am afraid," the small child said. "The Arab Turks are looting the islands and killing all the druids. I don't want them to come here."

"Go back to bed and sleep, my child," Elissa, the golden Sea Dragon, warmly conveyed in rich, velvet undertones. "We will take care of everything. Do not leave your village until the fog clears; then it will be safe again. Thank you for alerting us."

"Oh, you are welcome," politely replied the girl with a hint of glee and a slight curtsy. "I knew that you would help me. Thank you again. I knew that you could do it."

The little girl turned and hurried back to her hut in the village to do as the Sea Dragons had instructed her. She went back to her little straw bed and pulled the blankets over her to warm up from the chill. Very soon she was sound asleep and remained that way for several hours. In her dreams, she flew with the Sea Dragons over the world and surrounded the planet in a silver mist that kept it safe and protected.

Later in the day, Minerva, her elderly adopted mother, called her gently to breakfast. Joslin rose from her bed and washed before joining the aged couple at the table. They were childless, elder druids who had fled to Wales after the Pendragon seized their home in the Camelon Castle. They loved Joslin as they would have their own child. Her father had been the king of Camelon, and they gently guided her with patience throughout life's vicissitudes.

"What did the Sea Dragons tell you this morning?" the venerable gentleman at the table politely asked. He had risen early to split more wood for the fire and noticed that Joslin was out of bed. He had grown wise in his advancing years and understood the yearnings of young children, especially those who communicated with the Sea Dragons.

"They say that we will be safe and not to go outside of the village until the fog clears in the bog," Joslin replied without emotion.

"Oh, I see," the elderly woman nodded as she patted her life partner softly on the knee. She turned and gave him a knowing look. The entire village needed to be alerted so that they could also follow the Sea Dragons' instructions. Their subdued actions encouraged the small girl without causing her to feel self-conscious.

In Wales, those who didn't talk to the Sea Dragons listened to those who did. Life was too short. They clung to the lore surrounding the Sea Dragons while the other traces of their former civilization vanished all around them.

The Sea Dragons thrived in the imaginations of children aged two through seven. They had been responsible for the development of the mammalian brain after the Serpentines seeded the reptilian brain in the human form. The star seeds from the Noris cluster had been asked to intervene. They came to the planet as the First Pilgrims and enlightened the developing earthlings. They kept the earthlings underwater until they regained their former buoyancy and lightness of spirit. The Sea Dragons served the water spirits that parented this process. By the time the human form emerged from the sea, all the earthlings imagined that they were children of the Dragon.

After helping clear the table and clean the dishes, Joslin raced outside to watch the mist settle over the snow-covered village. The effect was like a blizzard, except there were no snowflakes. She remembered the stories that her father told her about the Sea Dragons. He would take her by the hand to the sea wall outside of the Castle Camelon and point them out to her. Sometimes the merpeople would catch rides on the Sea Dragons' backs and race through the waves. Sea Dragons could fly in the air too, but their scales were too slippery for humans to ride them like the Furry Dragons. The Furry Dragons served evolved land spirits, whereas the Sea Dragons represented evolved water spirits that resembled winged-fish. Both had managed to elude the Serpentine Federation, and their original form remained genetically intact. Other water spirits, like the merpeople, had been victimized by the Serpentines during Atlantis and became half-fish and half-human. Some of the merpeople mutated to a totally human form and were known as merwyns.

Joslin's father, King Arcas, had told her about his childhood friend, the Lady of the Lake. She was a mermaid who counseled him through his early years as king of Camelon. Likewise, Joslin adopted Earl and Elissa as her childhood mentors. Earl was the name of the garnet Sea Dragon, whereas the golden Sea Dragon was called Elissa. They had capsized many Roman ships intent on invading Camelon. The Greeks and Romans considered them sea monsters, but that was only a reflection of the monster within. If they had only been able to get a closer look, they would have realized that the Sea Dragons were exquisitely beautiful. However, if the Romans had possessed this profound attention to spirit, they never would have attacked Camelon.

Joslin wandered through the mist until she came to a clearing. There, in the middle of the clearing, stood Brunswick, the copper-colored Sea Dragon.

"I have something to show you," Brunswick communicated to her. He puffed up his chest and motioned for Joslin to hop on his back. He was wearing a makeshift saddle made out of seaweed, which his celestial caretaker had quickly crafted in response to Brunswick's demands that morning. O'Brunswick, the name of Brunswick's caretaker, cleverly fashioned anything the Sea Dragon needed for his job as world protector and record keeper. Sea Dragons remained very busy and required the skills of caretakers to see to their daily needs. These caretakers possessed the human form, which proved the most innovative. They lived in underwater sea caves that had air pockets. The Sea Dragons would dock at a pier in the sea cave and allow the caretaker to groom its scales. The caretakers also served the Sea Dragons meals according to their various tastes. Though most Sea Dragons knew how to forage for food, relying on their caretakers was more expedient. The human caretakers understood the omnivorous needs of the Sea Dragons best.

Joslin clung to the seaweed reins as Brunswick flew her to a small island off the coast of Wales. He gently landed on the rocky slope as waves crashed all around the edges of the island, which were only a few yards away on all sides. Joslin slid off the slippery dragon and stood beside Earl and Elissa, who were intently studying six small cocoons lying in a tide pool. Joslin noticed that several of the cocoons had cracks. Each cocoon was a different color, and the color of the wings could be seen through the cracks. The wings matched the color of the cocoon.

"Six tiny sea serpents are metamorphosing into Sea Dragons," Elissa, the golden queen Dragon, explained.

Joslin stayed for two hours while the Sea Dragons emerged from their cocoons like butterflies.

The blue cocoon opened first.

"I'm Gilderoy," the brilliant blue Sea Dragon announced as he shook his tiny blue wings dry. They were still wet with golden dew from the transition. Then Gilderoy kicked the green cocoon next to him with his webbed feet. "My friend here beside me is Marebell. You're it."

"That's not fair," a small voice whined from inside the green cocoon. "I'm not playing ocean tag with you anymore if you don't listen to me when I call a time-out."

"All right, you win," Gilderoy moaned as he looked at Joslin and shrugged. "Women!"

Elissa decided to intervene. A few puffs of steam emerged from her nostrils for emphasis. "Look, if you don't like it, grow fur. We are designated as a matriarchal society. It is called global balance. It is a tough job, but somebody has got to do it."

Earl wiggled his mustache when he heard her words.

"You tell him," squeaked another voice that was emerging from a breaking red cocoon. A little shiny red Sea Dragon stumbled out. "Gilderoy has been a pest. We must keep our focus to come out right. My name is Egraine. One of the intelligence operators at Camelon was named after me. I protected her parents when I was just a tiny sea serpent. They were so thankful that they named their daughter Igraine after me. She was a good friend of your father, King Arcas."

Joslin rubbed her small hands together in delight. "Oh, how nice to meet a friend of a friend of my father."

Egraine bowed gracefully despite her wet wings. "They put a statue of me as a full-sized dragon on the bow of their tiny wooden boat. They said that it was inspiration. Those Vikings needed all the help they could get in crossing the Atlantic. Their little boats leaked terribly." Pausing for a moment, Egraine surveyed her figure. "Looks like I made it. Just have to put on a little more weight."

"Ah, my dear, it is all in the crossing," sighed an elegant, velvet voice that was coming from a small opening in the violet cocoon. "Whether it is from the Norse land to the continent across the Atlantic or the snake to a bird, it is all in the transition."

"This is Neill," Gilderoy said to Joslin and the three mature Sea Dragons. "He is the philosophical one of the bunch. He was the last one tagged 'it.' He got caught conversing with the Asian sages."

Neill poked his violet head out of the opening in his cocoon and looked around. Then he answered for himself, "I was just whispering a metaphor to a man by the name of Tagore. What the caterpillar calls the end of the world, the master calls a butterfly."

"And puff, you were gone!" another voice sang, echoing inside a silver cocoon.

"That's enlightenment for you," Neill explained, getting his feet on the ground. "One minute you are playing ocean tag with a bunch of sea serpents and then you find yourself dispensing sage advice. Something changes and poof! You find yourself getting back inside the garden. Only this time the snakes are gone."

Joslin laughed and turned her curiosity toward the silver cocoon. It was beginning to smoke.

"Hello, Puff!" Gilderoy loudly announced. "Don't worry, he'll make it. He is not just smoke and mirrors. There is a little bit of a flame to him."

"He has got style," Marebell softly swooned.

Flames leaped into the air and Puff's cocoon vanished in a cloud of smoke. When the air cleared after a few minutes, a bright silver Sea Dragon rose up out of the ashes.

"Your scales hold up well," Egraine observed. "I like the stone in the middle of the forehead. Both Marebell and Neill have one too."

"It appears that three of the baby dragons formed cocoons while hiding in the Asian seas for ocean tag," commented Brunswick, the copper dragon, who also sported a pair of Viking horns on his capped head.

"Looks like Puff passed the flame test," Earl observed, wrapping one end of his mustache around a finger.

Elissa raised her golden, regal head and rolled her eyes. "Kids!"

Brunswick intervened. "OK, show is over. Time to get these baby Sea Dragons to their caretakers and to bed. They have a lot of growing up to do. It isn't all enlightenment, you know. Sometimes you just have to grow up." Then he shook his glistening head at Elissa and asked, "Do you mind taking Joslin back?"

Elissa welcomed the break from domestic duties. "Great idea. I'll take the scenic route back."

"Oh wait, this is for Joslin," Brunswick interrupted, handing her a golden staff. "You are the record keeper for the Sea Dragons. Since we keep records for everyone else, we request backup. Just wave it when you need to know what is going on or feel that you deserve an explanation. One of us will come running."

"Knock three times on the ceiling if you want me, twice on the pipes…" Puff sang with a little tap dance.

"Well, at least he is light on his toes," Elissa commented, who wasn't sure what to make of a singing and dancing dragon.

"He also likes to frolic in the autumn leaves," Gilderoy quipped. "That's why we call him Puff. He is as light as smoke."

"Oh," the golden queen dragon murmured before her attention turned to the smallest cocoon that remained in the tide pool. "Looks like we have a straggler. Let's stay a moment and see if he'll break through."

Everyone stared at the yellow cocoon. A tiny peep could be heard from inside it.

"Sounds like Conor is still breathing," Earl remarked when he heard the peep. "While we wait for Conor to make his way out, I want all the baby Dragons to finish eating your cocoons. It contains all kinds of magical nourishment to build powerful venom and hot breath."

Joslin sat and watched the baby Dragons munch on their cocoons. In many ways it reminded her of her mother, Laticia, who often gave new mothers dried placenta after childbirth. The dried placenta fortified the exhausted mother, and prevented most postpartum depression, and the babies thrived easier. Compared to the new mothers, the actions of the baby Dragons amused Joslin. Some practiced their fire-breathing skills in between bites. It was like watching a baby take his first steps, and the initial attempts at fire breathing were clumsy.

About five minutes elapsed before Conor appeared from his cocoon. He quietly stepped out of his broken cocoon, and immediately everyone realized the reason for the delay.

Conor blinked at the dragons and Joslin, and then he looked down at his two arms. Instead of paws, he had stubs. He shrugged a little and waved them softly in the air.

"Oh," the golden queen Dragon murmured for the second time that day. She turned toward the young girl studying the little Sea Dragon's deformity. "Joslin, it is time we get you back."

Queen Elissa waited for Joslin to take the seaweed reins on her back and then flew off into the mists. Joslin left the Sea Dragon queen after they landed in a meadow outside her village. She hurried back to her hut and grabbed a quick lunch. There was always a pot of warm soup on the wood stove by early afternoon. No one else was in the hut. She felt exhausted from her adventure with the Sea Dragons and lay down on her bed. Almost an hour later, she awoke to the music of a mouth harp outside. Joslin put on a warm sweater and wandered toward the music.

Wayne, her guardian and village chieftain, was playing the mouth harp a few yards away at the edge of the forest. He had a twinkle in his eye, and he winked at Joslin as he began a light-footed dance to accompany his music. Joslin watched, almost mesmerized. After a few short numbers, he stopped with a merry chuckle.

"I see that the Sea Dragons put you on staff," he said, finishing off his performance with a twirl.

Joslin thought that the village chieftain was as light on his feet as Puff the magical silver dragon. "They gave me a job as record keeper. They said that it was only fair that someone should keep a record of them."

"How many baby Sea Dragons do they have in their pod?" he asked her as he examined the nearby fauna for fairies.

"They have collected six. That makes nine dragons total," Joslin told him.

"More will come," he murmured as he bent over a fern. Something in the underbrush held his attention. He repeated his thought as if uttering a mantra. "There are at least two or three more cocoons."

Chapter Two

There is some reassurance

In going down together

As we be who we are

Tune Reference: *I'll Follow You Down*

----Gin Blossoms

THAT NIGHT EARL summoned Joslin in her dreams. The garnet Sea Dragon appeared much smaller than he was in physical reality and surfed the dancing white snowflakes in her dreams. He shone like a bright ruby-colored crystal drifting from the sky. When she awoke, she knew that someday she would learn how to sail the air with him. She hurried through breakfast and donned the warmest clothes that she could find.

"I am meeting Earl this morning," she told Wayne after he made sure that she ate a hearty meal. "I may be out for a while. I am not sure when I'll be back."

Wayne nodded his understanding before he advised her, "Stay warm. I'll see you tomorrow for dinner."

Joslin ran out of the hut and headed toward the place that resembled her dream the most. Snow fell from the skies when she entered the forest. She noticed a tree canopy that slowed the falling snow underneath a particular grove of trees. She stood amidst the trees and felt the silence of the moment. The area reminded her of the dream the most. A few seconds later, Earl emerged from behind the snowy mists. This time he was full-size, which amounted to a height of eight feet.

"I received your message last night," she communicated to him without words.

"Great!" he responded excitedly. Then he helped the little girl climb inside his pouch and flew away from the forests.

Joslin poked her head out from the pouch under his warm belly as the garnet Sea Dragon soared over the clouds. She soon became sleepy and burrowed inside a warm wool blanket that someone had placed inside the pouch. By the time she awoke, Earl had already landed on an island inlet off the coast of Wales. While she had been sleeping, he had gently removed her from his pouch and placed her in a small cave where several other children were sleeping around a warm fire.

Earl's caretaker handed her a cup of warm broth, and she sat upright from her sleeping position. The smell of warm food quickly revived her senses, and she studied her new surroundings. She counted seven other children with her inside the cave. Six of them had deformities and reminded her of Conor, the yellow dragon with the stubby arms. The children with the afflictions seemed fragile and weak. Even their cognitive skills seemed challenged.

The other child without special needs sat down beside Joslin and watched the rest of the group with her. Being a young boy with blonde hair and blue eyes like her, he remained quiet, occasionally glancing at the others.

"OK, time for introductions," Earl announced as he wiggled his mustache. "The arrival of Conor marks the beginning of a revised tradition. The new caretakers will be representatives from the local downtrodden communities, especially those that need a rebirth." Taking a deep breath, Earl resumed, "First, this is my new caretaker, Duke. He is learning how to talk, so please be patient with his sign language. Having been born in Scandinavia with a speech impediment, but he can now speak monosyllables."

Duke smiled and nodded at the group. He uttered a hoarse, "Yes."

Earl quickly changed the subject and introduced the next caretaker. He motioned to a young man brushing algae off the scales of Elissa, who remained docked at a pier a few yards outside of the cave. Elissa was scribbling notes on papyrus while her caretaker worked.

"This is Ellis. He was born deaf in Scotland, and slowly regenerating his ability to hear. He can hear low frequencies now."

Earl produced a small bass drum from inside a pocket in his pouch and began tapping a special code. Ellis stopped his work briefly and waved to the group inside the cave. Earl tapped a musical beat and began lightly dancing around the cave.

"Keep introductions short, Earl," Elissa warned. "I need my scales shined before I visit Tibet. I need to be able to reflect the sun so that I can blind any opposition."

"OK, OK," Earl responded. He stopped dancing and twirled his mustache. "Ellis, keep working," he spoke in deep tones.

"Now for the next caretaker," Earl continued. "Hey, O'Brian, can you see me?"

"Only in various shades of gray," answered a young woman who was busy sharpening Brunswick's claws with a large file, "but I see the light."

Brunswick looked up from the scroll that he was reading. "O'Brien has a great attitude. She sees with her fingers. I can't seem to get anything by her, unfortunately. She ruined my last practical joke I played on Elissa. She found the sea anemone that I put under Elissa's mattress."

"She did you a favor, Brunswick," Elissa, the golden queen Sea Dragon, retorted. "You know I am sensitive like the princess and the pea. I'm grumpy in the morning without my sleep. I would have burnt your breakfast for sure."

"*Getting back to our lesson for today*," Earl interrupted, creating a small puff of smoke to hide behind. "We have 'see no evil, speak no evil, and hear no evil.' So, folks, do we have evil?"

"Huh?" six children echoed around him.

"Just smile and respond, 'Yes,'" Brunswick interjected to the collection of children blinking at Earl.

Some of the children turned and looked at Brunswick and then at Earl. A few of them smiled, "Yes."

"Are we having fun?" Elissa questioned when the smoked cleared.

Some of the children smiled and nodded at Earl. "Yes," they said.

"Are you sure that Brunswick didn't put an electric eel in your mattress?" Earl asked in a loud, slightly irritated voice. "Give me a break. Don't you think that I have enough challenges right now?"

Some of the children smiled and nodded "yes" at Earl again. Seconds later all six of the children were smiling and echoing, "Yes."

"You just have to know how to talk to them," Brunswick replied. "They seem to follow my instructions very well."

The children looked at Brunswick and said, "Yes."

Joslin and her companion remained silent. They were not amused by the antics of the Sea Dragons under the dire circumstances. Now Joslin understood why the Sea Dragons needed someone to keep an eye on them.

"Ignore the copper-colored Sea Dragon named Brunswick," Earl instructed.

The children around him smiled. "Yes."

"Raise your hand if you had a dream about a baby Sea Dragon last night," Earl continued.

All six children smiled and raised their hands high in the air.

"OK, you there, little girl in the green dress named Donovan. Can you tell me the color of the baby Sea Dragon that you dreamed about last night?" Earl asked.

"Green," the little girl replied, "just like the color of my dress."

"Good job, Donovan!" Earl roared. Then he turned towards the back of the cave. "Marebell, please come out of cave number three."

A tiny green Sea Dragon came hopping out of cave number three. Marebell gave an impressive attempt at fire breathing, and her caretaker gave an impressive attempt at walking with a malformed right leg.

"Oh, she is so cute!" the child exclaimed as she rubbed her hands in delight and hobbled over to pick up the little Sea Dragon.

"Next!" Earl roared as the remaining children eagerly raised their hands for permission to speak. "You there, O'Conor in the yellow tunic. What color of dragon did you dream about?"

"The same color as the shirt I am wearing," the young boy replied, looking down at his tunic and pointing with undersized fingers.

"Conor, come out of cave number two," Earl shouted over his shoulder.

Conor sauntered out of cave number two. Without bothering to impress his audience with his burgeoning fire breathing abilities, he merely chose to hop in his new caretaker's lap.

You're color blind, aren't you?" Earl questioned.

The boy nodded as Conor snuggled in his lap.

"Just remember that your Sea Dragon's name is Conor and that he is yellow," Earl instructed.

"Now, Conor, don't go changing colors on us. You are not a karma chameleon," Earl insisted. Looking away at the sea outside the cave's entrance, Earl continued, "This brings me to another topic. Remember, children, we are dealing with dharma here, not karma."

The cave quieted. Conor lifted his head slightly before dozing off.

"We talked to all of your parents and elders in the communities before arranging to bring you here. Dharma is divine right action. The world has degenerated a bit since Camelon existed. Your special challenges are the key to getting the planet back on track. That is why we are here. Nine Sea Dragons have agreed to help take us to the next level. As you heal and transform your inherited afflictions, you will regain your power and use it to heal your communities. The Sea Dragons are taking over where our cousins, the Furry Dragons, left off. Because the Furry Dragons are endangered, many have taken refuge in MidEarth. It is up to us now to carry on."

Joslin listened carefully to the Sea Dragon's words. The other children picked up Earl's speech as if they were sponges. Though they didn't seem to fully understand what he was saying, they absorbed the sense of it. Many softly nodded their heads as if to say, "Yes," without realizing it.

Brunswick left his post and quietly whispered over Joslin's shoulder, "By the way, the boy next to you is your half-brother, Dadgon."

Joslin stirred and straightened in her seated position. She glanced at the boy next to her, who seemed five years older. The prospect of an additional family member who was still alive delighted her, though the complications weighed her down. Authenticity in relationships could not be forced. It dawned on her how in danger her birth parents had been. She shook her head a little to toss off her heaviness and stared at the boy again. He seemed not to notice; instead, he seemed absorbed by the scene before him concerning the Sea Dragons and their dharmic caretakers. Somewhere in his soul, Dadgon had found a fit.

"You and Dadgon are the new Dragon flyers," Brunswick explained in a hushed voice. "We are not as easy to fly as the Furry Dragons, but we will all learn together."

Joslin's eyes widened. She knew that her father, King Arcas, had started out as a Dragon flyer. Her mother had been a Dragon flyer but had given it up to become a physician. Arcas's parents, her grandparents, had been Dragon flyers as well. Events had come full circle with the promise of regeneration and renewal. She glanced at her half-brother again and sensed that she could accept him as a family member. She knew that her full brother was being groomed for leadership of the Turks, who accepted the promise of his reign like the Greeks' Trojan horse. Only she and a handful of others knew that the Pendragon's son was really King Arcas's son.

Brunswick went back to his post as Earl continued to ramble. "…And coming out of cave number one, we have Puff."

The silver Sea Dragon glistened in the smoke billowing from his cave. He proudly stepped alongside a boy whose face was deformed on one side. Named McDonnell, the boy wore a silver earring on the deformed side of his face. When the dragon stood on his unblemished side, McDonnell straightened and confidently puffed out his chest. The ruby stone embedded in Puff's forehead shone brightly and reflected a beam of red light in front of them.

"Next is Egraine. Come on out, Egraine," Earl bellowed. "I bet she belongs to the little girl wearing the red stocking cap in the back row. You must be Maclean."

Egraine flew out of cave number two and landed like a dove next to the girl with the red stocking cap.

"My dragon already knows how to fly!" Maclean cried. She was a pale, wispy ghost of a child. "And she is red! I always wanted a red dragon of my very own."

Then the little girl began to wheeze and have difficulty breathing. Earl looked concerned. Egraine rubbed the girl's back and softly cooed, "Just relax and let the world in. No sense getting all choked up over it. You can be free to breathe too!"

Maclean caught her breath as the red Sea Dragon fluttered in her face. She could not help but see directly eye-to-eye with Egraine. Looking at Egraine as she nodded, Maclean got her asthma attack under control.

"Our next Sea Dragon requires a firm hand. McGregor, you there in the blue tights and dark-blue dress, keep all of your six fingers and toes on this one. Yoo-hoo!" Earl called to the blue Sea Dragon emerging from cave number three.

Gilderoy threw his hands in his pouch and looked up sheepishly at Earl. Earl looked down at him sternly, and the blue dragon wandered over to the little girl dressed in blue. She assertively pulled him close to her and petted his slippery, scaly back. Gilderoy wiggled uncomfortably under all four of her thumbs but eventually softened with the direct attention.

"Last, but not least, we have Neill. Come out, come out, wherever you are, Neill," Earl yelled without bothering to direct attention to any particular cave.

Neill appeared out of nowhere and stood behind the boy wearing a violet bandana.

"He was behind me the whole time!" the boy shrieked in amazement. "He matches my bandana too! He even has a purple stone in his forehead."

The boy could hardly keep still. The focus he had managed to maintain for the session with Earl totally dissipated with the arrival of the violet Sea Dragon.

"I knew that O'Neill would be paying attention, so I saved Neill for last," Earl remarked to Joslin in a quiet voice.

O'Neill began roughhousing with the violet Sea Dragon, who quickly disappeared in the boy's pockets and shirtsleeves. Then Neill seemingly reappeared out of nowhere only to quickly disappear under some device. O'Neill seemed excited but perplexed. For a brief, shining moment, he paused in reflection before pursuing his masterful Sea Dragon again.

"Keep a close eye on that one," Earl commented to O'Neill. "The more you relax, the more Neill will allow you to see him. He doesn't like it when you move around so much."

O'Neill's high energy was infectious, and Earl relinquished control of the class to the tiny Sea Dragons and caretakers. "OK, kids and dragons, go frolic. After lunch we will discuss the basics of dragon care."

Earl mopped the sweat from his brow with a small towel from his pouch. "Let's have lunch together," he told Joslin and Dadgon. "The others will join us once they settle down and figure out that they are hungry."

Chapter Three

Be patient

As those who try

Work things out

Tune Reference: *Whataya Want From Me*

----Adam Lambert

AFTER LUNCH BRUNSWICK took Joslin back to her village. He landed in a small snow-covered thicket and accidentally sliced his paw on a nearby hawthorn bush. Joslin watched the red blood drip on the pure white snow and felt compassion.

"Looks like it is time to make opportunity out of adversity," Brunswick remarked as the blood dripped from his garnet hand. Then he turned toward her. "Are you sure that you want to be a Dragon flyer? Like your mom, dad, and your grandparents?" he asked her. "There is no turning back."

Joslin eagerly nodded. Dragon flying was in her blood. It gave her hope for the future. She would make it her world, just as her parents had done. Where else could she go?

The garnet Sea Dragon allowed some of his blood to drop on her open palms. "This will keep you from getting injured during flights."

Joslin immediately felt the skin on her palms toughen. A special magnetic quality began to emanate from her fingertips. When she placed her hand on Brunswick's back, she stuck to him like glue, but she could release her grip by using her will.

"The ionic compounds in dragons' blood interact with your skin to create an electromagnetic resonance. This is how to connect and disconnect from a Sea Dragon. You will no longer need to be strapped to our backs with seaweed. You'll soon learn that the best way to ride a Sea Dragon is barefoot."

Joslin stared at her boots on her feet. Although she loved going barefoot in the summer, she wondered how she would keep her feet warm during winter dragon rides in the frosty air.

"Don't worry. Your body will adapt naturally, and you'll figure the rest out," he assured her. He looked up at the sudden swirl of snowflakes dropping from the sky and into the thicket. He sighed, "Gotta get back to the inlet and get these young Dragons into shape."

Joslin watched the garnet Sea Dragon rise into the air and fly away in the white mist. She turned toward her hut in the village and sought the comfort of a warm hearth. Wayne, who was whittling a new wooden flute, looked up from the table. His partner, Minerva, was busily throwing together a soup for dinner. Both of her guardians watched silently as Joslin brought a stool in front of the fire, sat down, and stared into the flames.

"Met the young ones today?" Wayne asked lightly.

"Which ones?" she answered with a question. She was perplexed over the information that she had received today. "There were children a little younger than me and the baby dragons. They were all babies."

Wayne chuckled slightly as he continued carving and thought about her words. "Sometimes big things come in small packages."

"I know," Joslin agreed with a sense of wonderment. She released her gaze from the fire and briefly made eye contact with the people in the room. "I met my half-brother."

Wayne chuckled lightly again. "Your father never knew, but your mom figured it out shortly before she died. There's a half-sister too. Like your brother, Arthur, she's busy doing other things for the moment. It relieves the pressure. There are four children to share the challenges rather than just one or two."

"What did you mean when you said that more were coming?" she asked as she recalled his previous words.

"The baby Sea Dragons have other lost brothers and sisters. There are three more baby Dragons and caretakers making their way to the base at the inlet."

"How do you know?" she asked curiously. She began to understand why she had been placed with Wayne and Minerva. Wayne seemed to understand the wisdom of the generations as well as world history. "Earl and Brunswick never mentioned this."

"Well, being Sea Dragons, Earl and Brunswick have a lot on their minds, just like we do," Wayne said thoughtfully as he examined the flute that he was carving. "The humans were the shakers and movers during the time of Atlantis. The Sea Dragons were the only creatures that managed to avoid the Serpentine's experiments. They swarmed together in pods of twelve underwater. The disguised Atlanteans could not isolate a single sea serpent for the operating table.

"After the Great Cataclysm, a very powerful underwater wave carried three of the serpents to the Caribbean. They metamorphosed on their own and are making their way to the inlet to rejoin their pod."

"How do you know?" asked Joslin, who wanted to learn from Wayne as well as the Sea Dragons.

"The wild SeaHorses communicated this to me," Wayne said and returned his attention to his whittling. "They travel the Seven Seas regularly and saw the missing serpents sunning themselves in the tropics."

Wayne began to chuckle lightly again. "I don't know how those returning Sea Dragons are going to adapt to the colder Atlantic waters of this area." He stopped working briefly, chuckled again, and looked at Joslin. "Those big Sea Dragons could be in for a rude awakening. Some of the baby Sea Dragons may just want to go back to warmer waters."

Returning to his work as he sat back in his chair, Wayne instructed Joslin, "We gotta keep everyone together."

The next morning Joslin met the golden Sea Dragon queen at a snowy meadow outside the village. The snow came down so thickly that visibility was limited to ten yards around them. Joslin wore shoes that she could easily slip off and carry in her purse.

"Climb aboard, my child," Elissa encouraged her. "We have work to do. The other three baby Sea Dragons have been found. We must collect them and bring them to the inlet."

Without a word Joslin slipped off her shoes and scaled the slippery Sea Dragon with her bare feet. She wrapped her arms around the Sea Dragon's neck, and they left the meadow for the misty skies. Time passed quickly; Elissa swiftly sped through the skies and landed on a beach near present-day Morocco.

"Long time no see, my brothers and sister," Elissa said in greeting.

"Hey, you're looking good," Mansford remarked. He appeared as a tiny baby-blue Sea Dragon with clouds of white on his torso.

"There you are. You're a sight for sore eyes." Elissa kissed him on the cheek. "I like the camouflage. I can see why you've been so hard to find."

"It took us a while to get over the Serpentine trauma. Thank heavens Atlantis collapsed. It bought us time. We wanted to make ourselves scarce until the call came for action," Mansford replied.

"Where are the others?" Elissa asked.

"Here we are!" shouted two Sea Dragons who had been hiding in some nearby flowers. Both were decked in bright psychedelics and their colors blended with the flowers. One Sea Dragon had a paisley pattern and sported a gold jewel in the middle of his forehead.

"You're a trip, Paisley," Elissa observed.

"Thanks, Elissa," Paisley replied. He cautiously accepted the compliment. "You should check out Drummond."

Drummond grinned and changed his fluorescent psychedelic swirls to plaid.

"Well, it might work in Scotland," Elissa commented. "Can you tone down the colors?"

"That's the only issue," Drummond answered. "But at least the Scots will be able to find me in the night sky. I glow in the dark."

"That should scare the Serpentine Federation," Elissa sighed with a hint of sarcasm.

"It distinguishes us from them," Drummond insisted. "We are cool."

"Call it style," Elissa pondered with a touch of resignation. "Can you do something ferocious?"

"We can blind them with our colors," Paisley suggested.

"That's strategy!" Elissa observed. "It might work. The rest of us will need to wear shades, though."

"Or adapt," Mansford said.

"Point taken," Elissa replied. "Let's get going. There is no more time to waste."

Joslin helped place the tiny Sea Dragons in Elissa's pouch. Within seconds the group left the Moroccan beach for the inlet island off the coast of Wales. Time passed quickly, and they soon landed on the rocky beach outside the Sea Dragons' cave.

"We built a great fire inside the cave," Elissa told them as the tiny Sea Dragons hopped out and ran for the warmth.

"There's my Sea Dragon!" a child shrieked from inside the cave.

Joslin watched a little girl scoop up Drummond. She had a deformed spinal cord and a hump at the back of her neck. Somehow she had gracefully walked over to Drummond and elegantly directed him into her arms.

"Good job, O'Leary. That's the way to gently handle your Sea Dragon," encouraged Brunswick, who had taken over for Earl. "If he appeared in black and white, Drummond would look like a cow."

"Hey, wait a minute," Drummond interrupted Brunswick. "I'm the sky. Get it?"

Brunswick shook his head and ignored the tiny Sea Dragon. "Scott, come get your plaid Sea Dragon before he goes tropical."

Scott, the small boy in a plaid kilt, ran after Mansford. He bumped into another child on the way and fell on his knee.

"I can see him, I just can't focus," he explained. Mansford calmly stood near the fire and changed his psychedelic fluorescents from plaid to swirls like a flashing neon sign.

"I can see that we will go far together," Mansford said, winking at Scott.

Joslin giggled at the flashing Sea Dragon and bumbling boy, who also seemed to enjoy the show.

"This must be my Sea Dragon," a little boy observed. Having vitiligo, he picked at the white spots on his skin.

"Go for it, Murphy," Brunswick encouraged. "Don't let Paisley get under your skin."

"A little color does everyone some good," Paisley remarked. "Come on, Murphy, we have a lot to talk about."

"OK, party is over," Brunswick shouted. "Earl is coming."

"Hey, wait a minute," Earl insisted. "I AM the party. Anyone want to know a secret?"

All the children and baby Sea Dragons quieted.

"It is the secret of the Golden Flower, and we are going to learn how to open it," he said.

"Cool," Mansford said.

"All you have to do is sit down like this," Earl demonstrated, sitting cross-legged with his feet on opposite knees. "Curl your tongue under the roof of your mouth, close your eyes, and cup your right hand over the other with thumbs touching. Then empty your mind."

Earl assumed the pose and remained quiet for a half hour as the others mimicked him. Eventually everyone in the cave had figured out the position and sat silently around Earl. The three mature Sea Dragons, who had previously mastered the exercise, smiled as a gold light emanated from their faces toward the fire.

Fifteen minutes elapsed before Earl ended the mediation with another exercise set. The children and immature Sea Dragons awkwardly mimicked his actions. Earl ignored them and reclined peacefully on the sandy floor of the cave.

"I could use a nap," he observed while he gazed at the ceiling of the cave as if he was watching clouds in the sky. "Class dismissed. Go frolic."

Chapter Four

Let the generation

Of the damned

Give it a go

Tune Reference: *Take A Chance*

----ABBA

THE SEA DRAGONS taught the newcomers the chi exercises that they would need to open the Golden Flower. The baby Sea Dragons grew rapidly and within six months took a test flight with their caretakers. Another boy joined the group as a Dragon flyer so that all the mature Sea Dragons would have a rider. Being the same age as Dadgon, he had been Arcas's godson. People called him Eegan and he lived with Arcas's aunt and her life partner, Ed the Red Knight, in a nearby village. Eegan was the son of Merilyn and his counterpart Egressa. It became his task to lead the expedition to the mountains in Tibet so that each caretaker could retrieve a Golden Flower and bring it back to the sea cave.

For almost six months, the group had been doing the earth meditation that opened the Golden Flower in their mind's eye. Earl could determine when a child had mastered the alchemical exercise: he or she would radiate a golden light around the top of his or her head. This light served as a healing elixir for the practitioner. Each child's particular physical and/or mental challenge would begin to heal. Caring for the Sea Dragons imparted a special healing for each individual child. They served as modern-day exercises in *chi gung*. The earth meditation with the Golden Flower internalized the external healing interaction. By the end of the six-month period, all the caretakers were able to fly their Sea Dragons short distances.

Eegan possessed a special spiritual connection to the high, mountainous region in Tibet. Other people later knew it as Shangri La. Natives in India called it Shambala, whereas those in Siberia referred to it as Belovodia. Eegan just called it home and remained familiar with it through many, many lifetimes.

On the morning of the excursion, everyone boarded his or her Sea Dragon. Joslin rode Elissa, the golden Sea Dragon queen. Dadgon mounted Earl, the garnet Sea Dragon with the mustache, while Eegan took Brunswick, the copper Sea Dragon, by his horns. They flew high in the clouds and evaded detection by unsuspecting civilizations below. At this point in their development, the Dragon flyers had developed tiny scales on their hands and feet that enabled them to maintain a firm grip on their Sea Dragons. Some of the caretakers had started to grow webbing between their toes and fingers, which enabled them to clean submerged Sea Dragons. A few had even sprouted gills, which increased their lung capacity.

Eegan led the group to Flowery Meadow on the highest peaks buried in the clouds. The Dragon flyers dismounted and searched the array of brightly colored flowers for the golden, multipetaled lotus of their dreams. The Sea Dragons played and chased dragonflies in the Flowery Meadow while the Dragon flyers wandered. Within moments the youngsters congregated around Eegan as he quietly followed a glistening stream in the sunlight.

"My mother, Egressa, took me here when I was little," Eegan mentioned to Joslin.

After they had followed the stream for several yards, they came to a small lake with a waterfall. A man wearing a white tunic and leggings was waiting for them at the edge of the water. He had a gold sash around his waist and stood tall in tan leather boots.

"Call me Imaile," he said, grinning at the group before him. "Hi, Eegan. I see that you brought everyone."

"The gang is all here," Eegan replied with a smile.

Almost a hundred golden-petaled lotuses floated in the water behind the man in white.

"The Golden Flower of your meditation is here," Imaile told them as the children scurried past him for a closer look.

"Everybody has been working hard," Eegan explained. "They are very excited about seeing the real Golden Flowers instead of the one in their mind's eye."

"It is like having a dream come true," Joslin remarked as she carried her Golden Flower over to Imaile and Eegan. "Earl said that the worst thing that you could do to someone would be to take away their dream. Even worse than death."

"Now you have something far greater than the Golden Flower in your hand," Imaile commented. "It is the fulfillment of a dream, and that moment can never be taken away."

"How's Emaile?" Eegan asked.

"My teacher went to work in another dimension," Imaile answered. Then he looked at Joslin and told her, "Eegan worked with Emaile in a past life. That is why he knows these high mountains almost better than his home.”

“Time to get the Sea Dragons and go home,” Eegan announced, subtly changing the subject. “Imaile, it is great seeing you again. We gotta go. We are on a tight schedule. It’s time to usher in this next generation.”

The children wandered back to the frolicking Sea Dragons, whom they had left in the meadow. They were still mesmerized by the sight of the Golden Flowers in their hands. Carefully, the Dragon flyers put the Golden Flowers away in purses and pockets before boarding their Sea Dragons. The group soared high in the sky, and the aroma from the Golden Flowers permeated the atmosphere. The odor was almost intoxicating. Two of the Dragon flyers fell asleep and slipped off their Sea Dragons.

Joslin watched the bodies fall to the earth, but she felt too weary to cry out. The rest sensed the loss but seemed too numb to mourn. Nobody could save them. The fallen children seemed beyond anyone’s reach.

“They will die in their sleep and not feel a thing,” the queen Sea Dragon told Joslin as they continued their flight.

Joslin turned her head and saw a tear leave Conor’s eye. He had lost his Dragon flyer. She understood why the expedition to the high mountains of Tibet had been their test. Not everyone could handle the intensity of the energy. She noticed that the opiate effect of the experience faded as they neared the island inlet. If it weren’t for the Golden Flowers and missing caretakers, then she would have believed it had all been nothing but a dream. The excursion proved sobering. Joslin withdrew the Golden Flower from her purse and eyed it with respect. The experience had been a powerful one. She now understood the cost of the trauma that had hit O'Neill's and O'Conor's communities. The effect poisoned the subsequent generations.

Wordlessly, Brunswick took Joslin back to her village. In the middle of summer, the Sea Dragon left her in a clearing in the forest, and the vibrancy of the flora and fauna soothed her. The village loomed only twenty-five yards away, and she walked slowly as she reflected on the secret of the Golden Flower. The world of the Sea Dragons seemed only remotely associated with the world of her village, and yet a thread connected them. Raising her face to the blue sky above, she stared at the rays of sunlight falling on her village through the trees. This time she examined the sun with both her feet on the ground. The same sunlit sky that flooded the high mountains of Tibet and the bogs of Wales. She noticed that she had not changed either. Being more aware and more accomplished, and she found a different perspective that shed more light on her present mission. As she neared the village, she met Wayne, who carried a basket of apples to the hut.

"Come inside," he greeted her. "Here, sit down and have a fresh apple. You don't get them as fresh as this."

Joslin listened to the melodious cadence of his rather gruff voice and quietly followed his suggestion. Wayne entered the hut behind her and dropped the basket of apples on the table with an impressive thud. With a slight smile, he looked off in the distance, taking a moment of pride in the noise that he had made with the apples. The young girl studied the apples, and then he returned his attention to the goods in the basket.

"Here's a nice one," he told her, and he picked out a robust red one from the pile. His strong, brown fingers held the apple firmly in front of her eyes. It wasn't the sight of the apple that convinced her of its value; Wayne's gesture moved her to grab the apple from his sturdy hand. He gave her more than an apple that day: he offered her life. She shared his perspective after a long day spent searching for Golden Flowers and flying high above the clouds.

Finding an apple for himself, he began to whittle away at it as he had done with the flute. He dissected it in front of her while eyeing the story of its growth as he cut from skin to core. "These are good apples," he told her wistfully.

Somehow, in his manner she saw the golden sunlight captured in the fruit in his hands. He poured that sunlight for her as if he had brought it down from the skies himself. It was all there in front of her. The apple in his hands became the apple in his eye. Through his eyes, she saw the dawn of another day. It was as if he had opened the Golden Flower in front of her.

Wayne quieted when he had mesmerized Joslin with the basket of apples on the table.

"How many caretakers died today?" he asked softly. He seemed to understand the inner dynamics of life as if he was peering inside the mechanisms of a clock.

"O'Conor and O'Neill fell off their dragons," Joslin answered as she bit into her apple.

"No surprise there," he murmured softly. "Some wounds are so deep that it takes more than one generation to heal them. Their communities anticipated the loss under the circumstances. It is a harsh world and we must be prepared. The O'Conors and O'Neills are related to Bridget the Green Knight. The Fitzgeralds and O'Kennedys will take their places as caretakers. They are next in line as relations of the Green Knight. You'll meet them tomorrow."

Joslin continued eating her apple while he spoke. Its goodness soothed her sorrow and fortified her for the adventure ahead. Life went on.

"Go and play when you're done," Wayne encouraged in almost a commanding voice. "There's a group of kids at the river. They are racing small canoes built out of sticks."

Joslin hurriedly finished her apple and raced outside. Eegan had joined the group of children. They were making small boats out of sticks and racing them down the river. He, also, seemed to have left the earlier events of the day behind him. Later in the evening, all the children gathered around a campfire with the rest of the village. They sang and told stories until late at night. For the moment, their world seemed secure against invasion. Towards the end of the evening, Wayne came and joined the group around the campfire. He remained silent as he listened to the stories and fanfare. Joslin watched him absorb every word spoken, weighing it against his own knowledge. At some point, he shook his head and held out his hand for her to join him on the walk back to the hut. His gesture signaled that it was time to go to bed. Any more discussion around the campfire was not worth hearing. Delighted, Joslin placed her small hand inside his and rose up with a light skip beside him. She nimbly danced as they walked down the path towards his hut. He laughed and smiled at the lithe youngster at his side. Inside the warm hut, they bedded down for the night, and Joslin quickly drifted into a contented sleep. It was as if she had two childhoods. One pertained to the life that she had lived with her parents while they were alive. The second childhood involved the fairy world and the magical forests of Wayne and Minerva. The Sea Dragons encircled the periphery of this Welsh world with a penetrating mist that embellished every aspect of it. Somehow it all fit. She didn't mourn the loss of her parents; she felt that her childhood had migrated into another world, a very different and absorbing world, much like Wayne himself and his magical mystery tour.

Almost two weeks later, Joslin rode Brunswick back to the island inlet and met the new caretakers. She watched Fitzgerald and O'Kennedy clean the scales on Conor and Neill. Neither child had physical challenges. O'Kennedy battled with perpetual melancholy while maintaining a smile. Fitzgerald sang and danced to a fault, failing to complete the hygienic ritual of scale cleaning in a timely fashion. However, Conor did not seem to mind Fitzgerald's lack of attention, preferring to be entertained rather than cleaned.

"It is almost time for the rest of the Dragon flyers to arrive for training," Brunswick told her as he led Joslin around the inlet cave. "MacConor and McNeill come tomorrow to ride Conor and Neill. These young Sea Dragons have been working extra hard in training after the loss of their first caretakers. Neill is becoming very strong despite his missing limbs, which are beginning to slowly regenerate."

Joslin nodded her understanding, amazed at how the golden elixir of the secret flower found in the high mountains of Tibet healed people and creatures—as well as the altered states of the practitioners. This magic required both luck and dedication. In other words, it was an art as well as a science.

"Will the new caretakers and Dragon flyers be required to retrieve a Golden Flower from Tibet?" Joslin asked. She was concerned about losing more children who could not heal the wounds of their communities in one generation.

"No, it will not be necessary," Brunswick replied. "The groundwork has already been laid and alchemized for future generations. There is no loss."

The next day MacConor and McNeill arrived, flying Conor and Neill, but their introduction to the group in the inlet cave was quickly interrupted by the merpeople's underwater alarm system.

"There's a Roman army heading for a small island near Wales. They have been torching every Scottish village in their path. I think that we should teach them not to play with fire," Earl remarked to Joslin. He breathed some flames through his nostrils for emphasis.

The other Dragon flyers overheard his remarks and began climbing aboard the other four flight-worthy Sea Dragons. No time was wasted as they set sail for the skies. When they saw the Roman encampment below them, the Sea Dragons blew smoke in the air, reducing visibility in the camp to one foot. Then they laced the air with flames and torched the area. Soldiers cried out as they burned to death without ever seeing the source of the fire. Then the Sea Dragons and Dragon flyers quickly returned to the island inlet.

Joslin slid off Earl's back and glanced sideways at the other young Dragon flyers. A shudder went up her spine, and the other flyers seemed equally uncomfortable. Although, they had escaped from and survived many battles, this marked the first time that they had engaged in battle. The entire process of opening the Golden Flower had prepared her for this. The sheer enormity of the power slightly unnerved her.

Eegan shrugged at her. She felt much better watching his response. Dadgon stood with his chest lifted and stared into the distance. Having been raised at the Furry Dragon base on the Druid Isle, he saw the battle as a rite of passage that supported the legacy of a father that he had never known personally. The two boys' reactions, as well as the nonchalant manner of the Sea Dragons, comforted Joslin. It was an inevitable matter, of course. If they could preserve one piece of their magical world, then it would triumphantly radiate through the ages like the golden light of the flowers they had found in Tibet. Although King Arcas had won the war, there were still battles to fight and healing to be done.

"Please fly me back to my village," Joslin asked Earl.

Without a word, Earl knelt slightly so that Joslin could easily hop on his back. He flew her high above the island, into a peaceful sky under the changing hues of a melting sunset. By dusk, she had entered her familiar hut. Minerva remained sitting by the fire with her knitting as Wayne pulled a chair close to Joslin.

"Come tell us all about it," Wayne demanded in a nonthreatening but gruff voice.

Joslin sat down and stared at the fire. The charm of the village hut contrasted sharply with the reality she faced in the inlet cave. She swallowed hard at the realization. Wayne handed her a hot mug of spiced apple cider, and she slowly began sipping it. The brew warmed her insides, reviving her.

"You saw the smoke?" she asked.

Wayne eagerly nodded his acknowledgement. Minerva looked up from her knitting briefly and shrewdly eyed Joslin.

"We toasted an army of invading Romans," Joslin said. "They were not far from here."

"Gotta keep them away," Wayne commented as he brushed his thick arms across his legs in a sweeping gesture. It was as if he had wiped away the entire experience, causing it to dissolve in another world, far, far away from the inhabitants of the village as well as the minds of beasts and the children who flew them.

Joslin nodded quietly as she sipped from her mug. The cider made her feel sleepy. In a half-awake state, she began to drift into pleasant dreams about Flowery Meadows with bright golden sunrises.

"Time for bed," Wayne told her as he took the mug from her hand. "It has been a big adventure for you."

Joslin rose from her stool by the fire and curled up in her soft straw bed. She allowed the dream to carry her away into a deep sleep, where she literally awoke to the brilliant dawn of a new day. Slowly stretching while she rose, Joslin felt grateful that the night was over, at least for the moment.

Chapter Five

Make as many mistakes

As needed

To reach far away goals

Tune Reference: *Far Away*

----Nickleback

A WEEK LATER, Joslin met Elissa at the meadow outside of the village. The golden Sea Dragon queen looked more elegant than ever. The jewels embedded in her scales sparkled brilliantly in the morning sun. Her caretaker, MacArthur, had carefully groomed her over the last several days.

"How are you doing, my child?" Elissa greeted her sincerely in a soft, throaty voice.

"Fine," Joslin replied as she climbed the scales on the dragon's golden back. There was a renewed determination in her efforts to securely attach herself to the back of the Sea Dragon. This time she didn't slip.

"How is Wayne?" Elissa asked with an air of profound familiarity.

Joslin straightened herself on the back of the queen Sea Dragon and sat erect. Elissa's mention of Joslin's guardian surprised her. Suddenly the gap between the two distinct worlds of the village and sea cave had shortened with the connection that Elissa made with her inquiry. Never before had the

Sea Dragon queen referred to the village or even acknowledged that it existed.

Elissa read the child's thoughts. "Oh, Wayne and I go way back," she explained while she flapped her giant feathery wings and lifted her body in the air.

Joslin steadied herself as the Sea Dragon took flight. She had a feeling that the day would be full of surprises. Joslin patted the slippery golden scales on Elissa's back to let her know that she had been heard.

"You must tell me all about it when we land," Joslin told the Sea Dragon queen. Then she quickly changed the subject before the high altitude made conversation almost impossible. "Where are we going today?"

"The Druid Isle," Elissa answered in a hushed whisper. "It is time for you to meet the mother of your half-brother and half-sister, along with everyone else."

Joslin watched the earth disappear beneath the clouds as the Sea Dragon soared high in the sky. For a brief moment, Joslin felt euphoric at being above the troubles of the planet below and at the possibility of meeting people who had known her parents. Though she was hesitant to call the Druid Isle "home," she suddenly felt a connection that she had never known existed. Maybe it had in her seemingly distant past, before Camelon had fallen, but now she sensed a renewed bond, one that honored her present position.

Several hours later, Elissa broke through the clouds and flew through a heavy mist. Somehow, in the recesses of her memory, Joslin recognized the mist encircling the Druid Isle for protection. She could tell that Elissa was nervous as they approached the sandy bank of the island. Joslin pondered the cause for Elissa's anxiety. They slowly landed on the sand beside two adults.

"Hello, Joslin," greeted the tall man with the long white beard. "I am Gamaliel. This is Dadgon's mother, Queen Eilene. She knew your father, King Arcas, well."

A tear welled up in Queen Eilene's eye when she saw Joslin, who closely resembled her father. She knelt to the height of the child and met her at eye level. Lightly stroking the tiny scales on Joslin's right hand, she said, "It is very nice to meet you. Dadgon has told me a lot about you."

Dadgon popped out from behind a nearby bush. Joslin giggled when she saw him. She always appreciated his playfulness.

"You must come and meet my little sister," he announced, holding out his hand. He wanted to show her the Druid Isle that he enjoyed with his sibling and friends.

Joslin glanced at Gamaliel, who nodded with a wink. Eilene rose and waved them off with a smile. Elissa grinned and headed for the lake.

"Not so fast, my golden queen," Gamaliel remarked. "Please allow us to attend you after your long flight."

"No thanks, Gamaliel. You know what draws me to the water," the golden Sea Dragon queen answered in a serious voice.

"There is another survivor," Gamaliel yielded.

"Yes, and this particular merwyn will be more powerful than Merlin or you," the Sea Dragon queen reported.

"It is one thing to die from one's mistake, but it is another feat to return after another being's interference," Gamaliel replied with a slight gulp. He feared an inevitable shift of power with the arrival of Merilyn's successor. Wizards who transformed a death experience always returned several times more powerful.

Their conversation was interrupted by a sharp cry from the middle of the Druid Isle. "The Turks are coming!"

"Excuse me, Gamaliel," the Sea Dragon queen said as she turned around and headed for the old Furry Dragon base. "I have a battle to attend."

Joslin quickly emerged from the underbrush and lightly touched Elissa's face.

"The Turks are attacking the druid village across the river. They will want to conquer the Druid Isle next," Joslin explained softly to Elissa.

"I figured that it was only a matter of time," Elissa told her. "Climb aboard quickly. Earl will meet Dadgon here. The other three dragons will meet us in the clouds over the village. Their Dragon flyers are ready."

Joslin and Elissa left the Druid Isle and soared high in the sky. They flew above the cloud layer over the druid settlement. Minutes later, Eegan appeared beside them on Brunswick.

"Conor and Neill fly right behind us," the horned Sea Dragon told Elissa.

Joslin watched McNeill and MacConor emerge from the surrounding cloud layer within seconds. Their Sea Dragons, Neill and Conor, glistened in the sun. Their new caretakers, O'Kennedy and Fitzgerald, had groomed them carefully. Soon Earl and Dadgon appeared from the cloud layer. Earl had flown from the island inlet to pick up Dadgon at the Druid Isle.

The five Sea Dragons and their flyers swooped down on the Turkish army in a cloud of smoke. One of the Turkish soldiers raised his bow and arrow and shot Brunswick in the heart. The arrow found its mark, and Eegan skillfully landed the wounded Sea Dragon in a nearby thicket. Joslin and Elissa provided smoke for cover, which blinded the Turks to the possibility of a dying Sea Dragon on the ground. Meanwhile, Eegan tearfully said good-bye to Brunswick before mercy killing the Sea Dragon. Then he ran into an unoccupied tent in the Turkish encampment. Elissa torched the dead dragon to a crisp so that nobody would find the body and suspect the Sea Dragon attack.

"See what you can do on the ground," Elissa instructed as she flew away to torch some more Turks. "They will not suspect children but don't push it."

Joslin wiped away a tear and joined Eegan in the unoccupied tent.

"Why, you have become an old man!" Joslin exclaimed.

"The Turks fear old druids," Eegan explained. "My features age when I am outside of the druid or Tibetan camps. The ability came with puberty."

His words were interrupted by the shriek of a small child from an adjacent tent. Joslin and Eegan covertly went to peer inside the tent next door.

"It is the royal family tent," Eegan whispered. "That crying boy looks like he could be your brother, Arthur."

"Yes, that's him all right," Joslin observed in a hushed voice. "A crown and jewels are lying on the table across the room."

"That's King Gawain's stolen crown. They stole it after they killed him," Eegan commented.

Joslin eyed her little brother and straightened her jaw in determination. "I'll kidnap Arthur, if you can distract his nursemaids."

"I'll do better than that. I'll grab the crown jewels too," Eegan vowed as he tossed a candle in the corner where the nursemaids were napping. "I don't understand how anyone can fall asleep while sacking a druid village. Really."

"That's because the baby isn't theirs," Joslin answered as she crept near her sobbing brother.

Although he had never seen her before, he stopped crying and stared adoringly at her. Joslin had been with her mother during most of the pregnancy, though she had been given to guardians before the baby's birth. The small boy seemed to recognize her in a vague manner. He hurriedly crawled underneath the tent at Joslin's urging. Joslin picked up her brother and carried him to the site of Brunswick's ashes. She turned around and watched the smoke rise high into the sky from the burning tent.

"The baby! Where's the baby?" the nursemaids shrieked as they attempted to put out the fire that Eegan had started.

"Over here," Elissa cried to Joslin in a hushed voice.

Joslin followed the sound of Elissa's voice. She found the Sea Dragon queen waiting for her in the nearby woods.

"Let's get out of here," Elissa said as Joslin climbed aboard the slippery Sea Dragon queen with the child in her arms. Her scaled hands and feet firmly held her to the Sea Dragon as they took flight. Arthur glanced at the scene behind him and smiled at his older sister. Somehow he knew that he was going home. The Sea Dragon queen bypassed the Druid Isle and went straight to their base at the island inlet. When they landed, Joslin handed her brother to McArthur, Elissa's caretaker. Then she slid off the golden back of the Sea Dragon queen.

"C'mon, Arthur, let's go get a snack," Joslin told him as she took his hand in hers. She quickly led him to a wood stove at the back of the cave where Donovan was making some pancakes.

At the sight of contented small children gathered in the makeshift kitchen, Arthur relaxed and made himself at home. Joslin helped him get a plate of flapjacks with blueberry syrup. He noticed some of the other children eating at a table and sat down beside them on the bench.

"Can you keep an eye on him?" Joslin asked McDonnell, who happened to be sitting next to Arthur.

McDonnell quit eating for a few seconds and peered down at the small boy who had chosen to sit next to him. The only feature remaining of his former facial deformity was the silver earring. Arthur glanced up at the taller youth before taking another bite from his pancake. His blue eyes pierced the heart of the boy towering above him.

"Oh sure," McDonnell replied. "We're buddies."

McDonnell gently hugged the little boy next to him. Arthur nodded with a smile and resumed eating his pancakes with confidence. Then he straightened and mimicked the older boy next to him.

Satisfied, Joslin left the kitchen area and returned to Elissa.

"I sent Gilderoy to pick up Eegan," Elissa began. "He'll be a boy again when he returns." Then Elissa changed the subject. "This new boy looks like he could be your brother."

"He acts like he is my brother," Joslin answered. "He let me kidnap him."

"We have more Sea Dragons coming. The younger Sea Dragons collected six cocoons while we were gone," Elissa announced. "There is another urgent matter, though. We need to go back to the Druid Isle. There's a cave in the river that I need to find. One of the merwyns survived, and he is in that cave. A power struggle is about to develop between Gamaliel and the one that the merpeople call Merlin. He will be much more powerful than his predecessors."

Joslin looked at the rocky terrain underneath her feet and nodded her understanding. "We should leave at night to avoid being discovered. Although the mists will provide us with cover, the darkness always helps. I sense that Merlin needs to be away from Gamaliel's influence for many reasons."

Their conversation was interrupted by the appearance of Gilderoy and Eegan. Joslin rushed up to Eegan and hugged him. She felt relieved to see him in fine, youthful form again. He smiled at her as he dismounted from the brilliant blue Sea Dragon and handed her a cloth bag. Peering inside, she found that it contained the recovered crown jewels. She gasped and looked at Eegan and Elissa. Eegan continued to grin ear to ear while Elissa smirked. Gilderoy appeared indifferent.

"That should change history," Gilderoy remarked nonchalantly.

Elissa tossed her golden head back with a chuckle.

Joslin quickly changed the subject to more pertinent matters. "Shall we leave for the Druid Isle tonight? What about Arthur?"

Eegan looked around until he spotted the small boy alongside his newfound friends in the dragon cave. He appeared happy. Elissa studied the interaction between the small boy and the older children.

"He will probably drop off for a nap in an hour or so. He is getting tired. You can tuck him into bed and bunk him with the older boys. We'll be back by the time he awakes, so he won't miss you."

Eegan nodded his agreement with Elissa's plan. Joslin accepted her decision. She rested until Arthur had fallen asleep while listening to some of the older boys tell stories around the kitchen table. She collected him from the kitchen and carried her lightly dozing brother to a bed that had been prepared for him. She placed him in one of the bunks in the cavern before joining Elissa for the night flight. Eegan stayed, keeping watch on young Arthur and pondering what to do with the crown jewels for the interim.

Under the cover of a dark mist, Elissa and Joslin flew toward the Druid Isle and landed on a vacant island in the middle of the river. A merman popped his head above the surface of the water and greeted them.

"The entrance to the underground cave is a hundred feet south of the sandy beach on the Druid Isle. Go there and I will provide a covering mist for you. Don't land on the beach. Go directly underwater to the site. The sea creatures will light your way underwater. There is air in the cave. Joslin will not need to hold her breath for very long."

Elissa and Joslin dove underwater when they came near the Druid Isle. The glowing, phosphorescent sea creatures guided them to the entrance of a cave. Joslin held tightly to Elissa's back as she swam quickly inside the channel. When they noticed an air pocket above them, they surfaced. Joslin caught her breath on the subterranean beach. A trail on the beach led deep into a rock cavity.

"What is on the other end of the trail?" Joslin asked.

"It opens to another underwater cave beneath an island off the coast of Wales. It is where we found the other cocoons and Merlin."

Joslin followed Elissa into the darker recesses of the cave. Many questions crossed her mind as she groped in the black air behind the golden Sea Dragon queen.

"The waves on the shore at the end are too rocky to airlift a human," Elissa explained between breaths of fire. The fire from her lips illumined the cave temporarily so that they could get a heading. The fire breaths also provided some warmth and kept Joslin from shivering in the dark.

"Merlin has had a rough go of it," Elissa continued. "After falling into a nest of cocooning sea serpents, he fell unconscious. They saved his life and protected him from mental deterioration. Somehow he was able to connect with the sea serpents in his stupor and enlist their help. All the other merwyns drowned underneath the Serpentine's invading thought forms. With the help of Morgan Le Fey, the Federation drove the merwyns back into the water, where they forgot that they could no longer survive. The merwyns were all mutated merpeople, you know. The Serpentine Federation managed to invade their brain stems and make them think that they could swim like fish again."

Joslin shook her head as she remembered the tragedy. Raising her head, she relaxed as the dragon's fire sufficiently warmed the cave. The heat comforted her, renewing her spirit with hope. Joslin surmised, "So he is here."

"Yes," Elissa answered. "We need your help to reorient him. Although, he is very powerful, he is still vulnerable. The shock of regaining consciousness after such an ordeal makes him easily influenced. He needs to hang out with children and Sea Dragons until he regains his strength and complete cognitive abilities. It is as if he has had a rebirth, and we wouldn't want him to only be imprinted with the image of a Sea Dragon. It is hard enough remembering that he is no longer a fish. We need a human form so that you can mirror his present adaptation. Then he can figure the rest out."

For almost an hour, they wandered through the cave. The light at the end of the tunnel grew bigger and bigger. When they finally reached it, Joslin met a young, beardless wizard at the cave's opening.

"I sensed that you were coming," Merlin told them. "I could entrain to your brain in the alpha state."

"Good," Elissa replied in a soothing voice. "That's how it heals. We need to leave through the other end of the tunnel. It is too dangerous to fly you out of here. Not only are the waves more treacherous on this end, but also the Romans are watching the cave's opening from their ships. Now is not the time for close encounters of the third kind. Not until your conscious identity settles."

Joslin took Merlin by the hand and tucked him in line behind Elissa, who had already turned and breathed fire into the cave, lighting the first few feet ahead of them. Merlin glanced at the little girl beside him and slightly smiled. Her presence reassured him and illumined the dark crevices of his own mind. He stepped behind the golden Sea Dragon queen with renewed confidence as they slowly made their way back inside the underground channel. A small group of merpeople was waiting for them on the other side. They guided the swimmers to the island above the underwater channel. At the beach, Merlin joined Joslin on Elissa's back, and they flew in the dark mist to the Sea Dragon's cave. Eegan met them after they landed. He greeted and attended to Merlin, and Joslin slipped away from the welcoming party to check on her sleeping younger brother. The small boy had scarcely stirred from the original position she had left him in. Gazing at his peaceful face, she examined his calm surroundings in the bunkhouse cavern, which was quite a change from the tent with the Turks. He seemed to feel at home here. Eegan joined her moments later.

"What are we going to do with Arthur?" Eegan asked her.

"Well, he is a lot like Merlin," Joslin remarked softly. "He seems to be able to track energy for adaptation. It is odd that they should come back at the same time. Almost like twin souls. I think that they both need me for the moment. I'll be living in the Sea Dragon cave for a while, though I miss my home with Wayne and Minerva."

"Well, you can always come visit me in the high mountains of Tibet," Eegan commented. "Now that Brunswick is dead, I am a Dragon flyer without a dragon."

"Yeah, well, just remember that out of Brunswick's ashes came a rebirth. That dragon helped even from the other side. There's no time to grieve or be sad over his death. The circumstances led us to Arthur, the crown jewels, and Gawain's stolen crown."

"Then there is the appearance of Merlin and more cocooning Sea Dragons," Eegan added with a mild sigh. "Signs of new life are all around us."

Chapter Six

Sometimes the challenges

Are overwhelming

Tune Reference: *Seasons In The Sun*

----Terry Jack

THE NEXT DAY Elissa approached Joslin at the kitchen table.

"We have another mission," the golden Sea Dragon queen told her.

Joslin finished placing some biscuits on Arthur's plate and looked at the golden Sea Dragon queen.

"I dreamed about it last night," Joslin replied. "What is going on?"

Arthur happily munched on a few of the biscuits as he listened carefully to the conversation between the Sea Dragon and his sister.

"We need to pay a visit to Nimue. Her son is about Arthur's age now, and the Marlboro Castle is in danger. We may need to airlift another young boy," Elissa explained.

Joslin leaned toward her younger brother, who beamed under her attention.

"Will you be all right if I have O'Kennedy and McDonnell look after you?" Joslin gravely asked her brother. "Remember to cooperate with them."

Arthur bounced on the bench with delight. Somehow he sensed the importance of his sister's activities and was proud to be associated with her.

He loved being with his closest adopted playmates O'Kennedy and McDonnell, who were like older brothers to him. Arthur desperately wanted to belong, having enjoyed a new sense of purpose in his youthful life. He nodded at Joslin as he ate another biscuit.

"OK then," Joslin agreed as she patted his small shoulder. "I will see you when I get back."

Joslin rose from the table and strode over to where O'Kennedy and McDonnell were attending their Sea Dragons.

"Keep an eye on young Arthur here," Joslin instructed them. "He looks up to you both as role models. I think you have a fan."

McDonnell winked and smiled at Arthur. "When you are done with breakfast, we need your help cleaning up Puff and Neill."

Arthur heard McDonnell and quickly began stuffing the remnants of his biscuit in his cheeks. Joslin and McDonnell noted Arthur's excitement and chuckled between themselves.

"Hey, but I need Arthur to help me with MY DRAGON," O'Kennedy interjected as he looked up from shining Neill's scales. "I gotta get the brine off Neill before he smells like a fish."

Arthur lost his patience and hopped from his bench at the table. He hurried over to the group just as Joslin decided to leave. He had a biscuit in his pocket and his cheeks were enlarged with the one left in his mouth. McDonnell waved Joslin off and handed Arthur a sea sponge.

"I see that you are excited to get to work," McDonnell observed. "Puff is a very gentle Sea Dragon, but he gets particular about how he likes to be sponged. Go in smooth vertical strokes like this. Don't disturb him. Sea Dragons are very busy creatures, you know."

McDonnell showed Arthur how to sponge Puff, who was busily practicing his fire breathing aim. He paid no attention to the small boy. Meanwhile, Arthur ran his tiny fingers across Puff's silver scales like he was petting the soft fur on a cat. He became absorbed in his work, taking care to not disturb the busy, silver Sea Dragon.

Joslin met Elissa at the entrance to the sea cave. Her caretaker, McArthur, had done a very good job of polishing her golden scales. She shone brilliantly in the sunlight, and the people around her were almost blinded by her reflection.

"Let's go to the Castle Marlboro," Joslin said as she climbed on the back of the Sea Dragon queen. "Arthur needs to play with someone his age."

"Yes, and so does Nimue's son," Elissa commented. "A castle under siege is not a great place to play safely."

The Sea Dragon queen lifted her mighty wings and soared high in the sky. Joslin held the back of the Sea Dragon tightly. She had not been to England since she was almost Arthur's age.

"We'll pick him up at Stonehenge," Elissa said. "They call him Gareth."

They flew over seas, forests, plains, and rivers until they came to the familiar thatched dome. The Sea Dragon queen landed at the entrance. Several knights came out of the shataquah to help them with their mission.

"Forces from Constantinople are attacking the Castle Marlboro," one of the knights said. "They are penetrating the secret rooms where Nimue and her court are hiding."

He lifted a small boy onto the back of the Sea Dragon. Joslin placed him in front of her and secured his position.

"You know how to reach us if you need to contact Gareth," Joslin reminded them as Elissa turned and headed for the skies again. "Time for him to learn how to fly Sea Dragons."

The knights waved farewell and hurried back inside the shataquah at Stonehenge. Joslin turned her attention to flight maneuvers. Out of the corner of her eye, she spied enormous legions of Roman soldiers marching toward the Castle Marlboro north of the Stonehenge shataquah. She felt a sinking sensation in her stomach. Her gut instincts told her that this would be the last visit to the Marlboro region for a while. Glancing down at the small boy on her lap, Joslin noticed that he had seen the army too. Gareth dropped his jaw slightly as his face became ashen. She held him firmly in her arms and gave him a gentle hug. He looked up at her in appreciation of her subtle gesture.

"There is a boy your age at the cave," she reassured Gareth. "I think that you will like playing with him."

Gareth took a deep breath and steadied himself on the back of the golden Sea Dragon queen. Then he resolutely looked forward into the mists beginning to envelope them.

Joslin and Elissa landed at the mouth of the sea cave. O'Kennedy and Arthur ran to greet them. Arthur saw the boy was his own age and rubbed his hands together in awestruck delight. Gareth noticed Arthur and offered a shy grin as he tried to climb down from Elissa's back in a manly way. Joslin watched the four-year-old boys gravitate to each other and then stand back from their introductions. Each boy eyed the other curiously and cautiously. Elissa glanced at her as Joslin wiped a tear from her left eye. There was much happening too fast.

Joslin noticed Elissa's attention and stepped farther away from the crowd forming around the little boys, who were still sizing each other up.

"I miss Brunswick," Joslin admitted.

"Me too," Elissa answered softly. "Though, he is not the only one or the only thing we miss."

Tears escaped Joslin's eyes as she buried her head under Elissa's right wing. The Sea Dragon queen nuzzled Joslin's wet cheek.

"I am happy to have my brother back. Mom and Dad would be happy to know that he is where he belongs," Joslin remarked.

"Yes, he will be happier here, though the Turks will claim him as their own king," Elissa sighed, recalling how Joslin's mother had hidden her pregnancy and passed the newborn off as the Pendragon's heir. It had been no small feat, but she had managed to fool the Pendragon and his peers.

"Much has been returned to us, despite the surrounding tragedies," Elissa murmured. "Let's go get something to eat and celebrate our wins."

Joslin dried her tears and raised her head. Earl, the garnet Sea Dragon, hurried toward them.

"You must see the new nestlings. You've never seen so many different colors in one batch."

Elissa smiled. "Thanks, Earl. The baby Sea Dragons will have to wait until Joslin and I have recovered from our journeys. We'll be at the nest after a bite to eat and some rest."

"We'll take it from here," Earl answered as he hurried back to the nest like a proud father.

The next morning, Arthur tugged at Joslin's nightshirt and woke her up.

Joslin stirred and blinked her eyes at the small boy. He held a hot pink baby Dragon in his tiny hands.

"I'm gonna be a Dragon flyer just like you," Arthur told Joslin as she sat up. "My Sea Dragon is pink. His name is Alfred. Devon takes care of him. Dadgon says that all the new caretakers are village idiots. What is an idiot?"

Joslin rubbed her eyes and shook her head at all the information hitting her this early in the morning. She gazed at the hot pink dragon singeing the edges of Arthur's tunic.

"Alfred seems to be a hot little guy," Joslin observed.

"Yes, he'll keep me warm at night," Arthur replied nonchalantly. "So what are idiots?"

"People who like to keep things too simple," Joslin answered, stroking the scales on the back of the hot pink Sea Dragon.

Chapter Seven

The reality checks of our lives
Reminds us that we are on our own
It's our own gambit

Tune Reference: *Second Chance*

----Shinedown

JOSLIN TOOK ARTHUR by the hand and went to see the new baby Sea Dragons.

"Most of the new ones arrived in radiant pastels or fluorescents," Earl explained, twirling his mustache contemplatively. "We must use them discriminately on the night flights. They all glow in the dark."

"It is going to be interesting," Joslin commented as she peered at the baby Dragons and new caretakers. "Have you seen Eegan?"

"He went back to his home in the high mountains of Tibet," Earl answered. "He decided to take a mini-vacation before wandering the Scottish countryside."

"Will he be back soon?" Joslin asked. She already missed his presence.

"It will a month," Earl answered.

"I want to go back to the village and introduce Arthur to Wayne. I could use a mini-vacation too," Joslin suggested.

"That's sounds like a wonderful idea to me," Earl remarked, twirling his mustache again as he cocked his head from side to side. "Get back into the village scene."

"Great. I'll go pack up a few things and meet you at the beach," Joslin said. Then she turned her attention to Arthur. "How would you like to go to a real village and meet Wayne and Minerva?"

Arthur looked at her curiously. She saw a hint of the longing for a boyhood home in his eyes. He quietly nodded.

"Let's take Alfred back to Devon so that he can finish grooming him while we are gone. Alfred will be fine. Your pink Sea Dragon will grow big and strong under Devon's care."

She took his hand, and together they scouted the cave for Devon. They found him resting in the sea cave's bunkhouse.

"Take good care of Alfred," Arthur instructed Devon as he placed the pink Sea Dragon at the foot of his bed. "He's my friend."

Devon nodded his understanding, assuming full responsibility for the treasured hot pink Dragon. Meanwhile, Alfred continued practicing his fire breaths with renewed confidence. A flame reached the edge of Devon's bunk and singed his blanket.

"He's a hot one!" Devon observed as he put out the ember. He was delighted by his Sea Dragon's skill and determination. Devon was a young man who admired action. He quickly waved off Alfred and Joslin and reassured them that Alfred was in good hands.

Earl took them to the village in Wales and dropped them off. Joslin took Arthur directly to the little hut where her adopted parents lived. She opened the heavy wooden door, ushered Arthur inside, and greeted Wayne. He seemed to be waiting for her by the hearth. Without rising from his chair by the fire, Wayne smiled with a lighthearted chuckle and motioned for the children to sit down by the fire.

"I see that you brought your brother," he acknowledged. "We've been keeping watch on the Pendragon's heir since his birth. Minerva made an extra bed for him next to yours."

Joslin's jaw dropped slightly and she blinked. For the first time in a long while, she felt whole and complete. Wayne had a special talent for bringing people together in so many ways.

"He has a Sea Dragon too," she told Wayne.

Arthur nodded confidently at Wayne as he sized up the gentleman. Then he sat down between Wayne and Joslin as if he had known Wayne all his life. Without bothering to respond to their conversation, he merely added, "My dragon is hot pink."

Wayne stared down at the small boy making his acquaintance and laughed. He winked and smiled at Joslin.

"The new ones glow in the dark," Wayne stated as he glanced at Arthur.

Joslin smiled at Wayne's acceptance of the newcomer who was making himself at home as quickly as possible.

"Did you get something to eat?" Wayne asked, getting down to the business of adopting Arthur. "Minerva made a big pot of stew. Here, come sit down at the table and get some dinner."

He rose and headed for the pot of stew before the children had a chance to think it over. Lifting the cover of the pot, he inhaled the aroma with an exaggerated gesture. The children watched him briefly and then gathered around the table as if enchanted. After placing bowls and utensils on the table in a matter-of-fact manner, he filled the bowls with stew and pushed them under Joslin and Arthur's noses. They hungrily ate their portions as he joined them at the table with his own bowl.

"Eat your food," he told them as he eyed Arthur with encouragement.

Joslin watched Arthur obediently devour his food without fuss or hesitation. She watched Wayne break off a piece of bread and dip it into his stew. Satisfied that Arthur was getting the nourishment that he needed, Wayne turned his attention to Joslin.

"The ogres are coming to town tomorrow," he told Joslin.

Without speaking, Joslin shot Wayne a quizzical look.

"Merlin is bringing them from the Arctic Circle. They were hybrids from the Serpentine experiments. They are a little gruff, but their hearts are in the right place. They work hard."

Joslin pondered this latest piece of information as she stared at her stew before taking her next bite.

Wayne eyed her as if letting her in on an inside joke. "Merlin is going to settle them around Stonehenge. The Romans will have to get past the ogres to get to Stonehenge. We need to put Stonehenge in another dimension. The ogres are so base that the Romans won't be able to even think after encountering them."

Joslin grinned. There was nothing more frustrating than trying to have an uplifting, reasonable discussion with an ogre. The unsuspecting Romans did not know that they were in for a very frustrating experience. They would not be able to even lace their sandals after talking with an ogre.

Arthur had fallen asleep at the table during their discussion. "Let's get this little one to bed," Wayne suggested quietly when their conversation had subsided. "I'll take your bowl."

Joslin rose from her chair as Wayne cleared the table. She lifted Arthur across her shoulder and carried him across the room. She placed him in the alcove bed next to hers and covered him with several blankets. He stirred as she removed his boots, but he never fully awoke. Then she went back to help Wayne clean the dishes.

"I miss this place," she said as they dried the dishes and put them away. "Looks like Arthur feels at home here."

Wayne took a step back and continued drying the mug in his hand. He chuckled with a slight shrug. "It's a nice home."

Joslin finished drying her bowl and announced, "I think that I will go to bed too. I am exhausted. There's a lot happening at the dragon cave."

Wayne watched her leave as he tidied the kitchen area. Then he went outside to sit and gaze at the moonlit forest. It was his favorite thing to do in the evening. Joslin often found him rocking in a chair on the porch and staring off into the distance. This activity seemed to relax him, and she enjoyed hearing about his thoughts on life. All she had to do was sit down beside him and he would share his observations about the world with her. They flowed as easily and smoothly as the motion of his rocking chair and as brightly as the twinkling stars in the sky.

Joslin slipped into the bed next to Arthur's and fell into a contented sleep. The light of the universe filled her consciousness, and she awoke refreshed. Arthur had already risen and was talking to Wayne as they prepared for a fishing trip. Joslin overheard his youthful voice and smiled at their rapidly developing friendship. She met them in the kitchen area, where Wayne greeted her with a cheerful smile.

"The fish in the river are calling," he explained with a sparkle in his eye.

"Wayne is taking me fishing," Arthur exclaimed with delight and a little bounce in his step.

Joslin gave Wayne an appreciative smile. She had wondered how to fit her younger brother into her life, and now she had her answer.

"I'll be meeting Earl this afternoon," Joslin offered. She had dreamed about the garnet Sea Dragon and knew that it was time to leave the hut again. There was a mission concerning activities on the Druid Isle. Her own Sea Dragon, Elissa, would meet them there.

Wayne solemnly nodded at her. "I talked to Earl in the meadow early this morning. He is waiting for you."

Then he turned his attention to the small boy jumping for the fishing pole that he dangled in front of him. Arthur caught the pole in his arms and proudly displayed it to Joslin. Seconds later he quietly followed Wayne out the door with a little skip. Joslin laughed at their subtly comical routine; then she prepared for her journey to the Druid Isle. The dream that she had had last night fed her thoughts as she hurried to the meadow to meet Earl. The theme of the dream revealed that the mission pertained to the water supply on the Druid Isle.

She met Earl at the meadow and climbed up his slick scales. Her bare feet and fingers gripped the Dragon tightly with the magnetite in her own soft, shimmering scales. When she was secured on his back, he took off.

"Some of the younger Dragon flyers on the Druid Isle have been drowning in the same manner as the young merwyns did. Both Gamaliel and Queen Eilene are acting strange. Elissa wants to do an undercover investigation."

Joslin nodded her understanding. It reminded her of her dream during the previous night. She had seen the vapor of a dark cloud permeate the wells on the Druid Isle. When she peered into the dark abyss of the well, all she had found was an orange crystal at the bottom. A woman came to the well as she peered into the darkness at the glowing crystal. She had been a former trainee on the isle and had left under mysterious circumstances. In the dream, Joslin turned her attention from the well to the woman on her right. When their eyes met, the woman laughed at her hideously. Then the woman turned into a black vapor resembling the cloud that had contaminated the groundwater.

"Has anyone ever quit being a Dragon flyer?" Joslin asked as she recalled the details of her dream.

"There was one trainee who left two years ago," Earl answered. "He left suddenly for unknown reasons. Nobody really understood why. The Druid Isle was busy recovering from a close attack at the time."

"Could he have been a traitor?" Joslin questioned.

"Most likely," Earl replied.

When they landed on the sandy beach, Elissa emerged from the heavy mists. Visibility was only two feet, and they remained undetected by the inhabitants on the Druid Isle.

"I requested that the merpeople shield us under a cloak of mist while we investigate," Elissa explained.

Several seconds later, Merlin appeared from the mists.

"There is still a connection between us," Merlin announced as he glanced at Joslin and the Sea Dragons who had saved him. "I've come to help and get to the bottom of this. It would be therapeutic."

The Sea Dragons just stared at Merlin, who had started to grow a beard on his baby face. Joslin nodded at him with a shrug.

"I think that we should look for water contamination," Joslin began. "Maybe somebody infused a crystal with a negative frequency that adversely affects theta brain waves of certain DNA sequences."

"You are beginning to sound like your father," Earl remarked. "Where did you learn radio theory?"

"I helped him on the Avebury shataquah before it was moved to Stonehenge," the young girl answered. "Someone should check the reception at Stonehenge for interference patterns."

"Earl," Elissa said, "how about taking Merlin to the shataquah at Stonehenge and see what he can find?"

Earl bowed gallantly at the request. He was delighted at their progress.

"By the way, how did you get here?" Elissa asked Merlin.

"Oh, I have been hiding on the Druid Isle. I figured that it would be the last place that Gamaliel's group would look for me." Then he added, "I also gained insight into their recent operations and refreshed my memory on things I had forgotten. They are really off. If they had any brain waves left, they would have detected your presence like I did."

"You have a point," Earl remarked. "They have truly lost their connection with us."

"Either that or Merlin's connection is more solid due to the circumstances of the rebirth."

"Now that could be..." Earl pondered as he twirled the end of his mustache. "C'mon, Merlin, we have a job to do."

Merlin hopped on the back of the Sea Dragon and Joslin tied him down with a spare rope that she always carried for emergencies. Then they took two steps forward and disappeared into the mist. Elissa stared wistfully after them for a few seconds and decidedly said, "Let's find what might be degenerating the brains of those on the Druid Isle."

"Do you remember the trainee who left after the last attack?" Joslin asked.

"Yes, I remember him well," Elissa said. "Do you think that he might have contaminated the water supply?"

"We can check," Joslin offered, glancing toward the heart of the druid village.

"No, let's check on the older wells first before risking exposure. I don't feel like explaining myself to Gamaliel yet. There is a well outside of the village that was abandoned after the last attack. People regrouped and the well was no longer used as much. The timing fits the suspect. Let's fly there; otherwise I leave too much trampled vegetation behind me. They would know that a Sea Dragon came to visit. All the well-beaten paths to the old well have vanished in the underbrush."

Joslin agreed and quickly boarded the Sea Dragon. They spotted the old well hidden amongst overgrown vegetation. Joslin slid off the golden Sea Dragon and tore the brush away from the well while scouring the area for clues. She noticed a strange orange light reflecting off the stones near the well. The reflection pushed her a step back like a puff of smoke in her face. Elissa watched her reaction to the orange hue, and her eyes widened.

"I think that we have something here," the golden Sea Dragon queen said. "There's is the old symbol for the Serpentine Federation carved on the stone closest to the bucket. You probably would not recognize it. Only the celestials and time travelers know it. It would have eluded Gamaliel, including his predecessor and successors."

Joslin looked at what Elissa's golden-scaled finger was pointing out. There, on the brick next to the bucket, was a carving of the eye of Horus over a pyramid-like structure.

"I've seen this symbol before," Joslin remarked.

"The Time Wrinkle that trapped your father and his soldiers came from this period of Earth's history," Elissa explained.

"I thought that the symbol was used for protection," Joslin commented.

"It depends on which side that you are on," Elissa insisted. "The eye of Horus refers to the eye in the sky that manipulated the earthlings. That connection was destroyed when three insurgents destroyed the crystals in Atlantis. True, the crystals and the electric eye were protective, but it came at the price of individual freedom. Some call it a codependent relationship."

"So in our dream states, we reclaim our power in a process of individuation," Joslin observed. Her dreams had led her to the contaminated well affecting her universe."

"That's where the Sea Dragons come in," Elissa announced.

Chapter Eight

People appreciate it

When you tell the truth

And don't fake it

When life gets complicated

Tune Reference: *Complicated*

----Avril Lavigne

JOSLIN PEERED AT the bottom of the well. She saw several stones glistening in the moonlight, their reflections bouncing off the water vapor around them.

"I see a crystal that might be causing the problem," she told Elissa, who joined her side and looked into the well.

"I'll lower you inside with the spare rope inside my pouch," Elissa suggested. Your connection with the Sea Dragons will protect you if needed."

Joslin retrieved the rope and knotted it around herself. Elissa lowered her down the well, and Joslin used her handkerchief to pick up the crystal with the black spot in the middle.

"This stone casts an eerie irradiance," Joslin commented after she had climbed out of the well. She produced the stone from her purse and unwrapped part of her handkerchief to display it.

"Good choice," Elissa encouraged. "Let's take it back to the cave for further testing. I want to be sure that we have correctly identified the problem. If removing it is the solution, I want to be off the Druid Isle before Gamaliel and Queen Eilene come to their senses. I don't want to have to explain anything that I don't fully understand myself."

Joslin tucked the stone back into her purse. Together, she and the golden Sea Dragon queen flew over the mists. They landed at the Sea Dragon cave, where Merlin met them.

"That was a quick trip to Stonehenge," Elissa accosted the burgeoning wizard.

Earl appeared from the deeper recesses of the cave and intervened.

"They had already attacked Stonehenge," Earl said pointedly. "We turned around mid-flight so that we would not get caught up in the fray."

"The energy still remains in the dimension that I placed it, but it will be thousands of years before the globes stabilize enough for it to manifest on the physical plane again," Merlin interjected.

Elissa buried her regal head in her golden-scaled hands. Joslin looked quizzically at Merlin and Earl. They didn't seem as worried as Elissa.

"The good news is that the frequency of the destruction was found all over the site," Merlin explained.

"We could get it from the air," Earl said, twirling his mustache. "We recorded it with Merlin's portable listening device."

"I was experimenting with it before I lapsed into the semiconscious state," Merlin explained.

"OK, take it to the auditory test room with the crystal that we collected from the well," Elissa directed Merlin and Earl. "I want all three frequency signatures compared. See if the deaf caretakers can pick up the signal; it may be part of the cause of their deafness. They can't hear anything else due to interference."

Joslin interrupted the scene. "Can I get a flight back to the village? I want to get back home and check on Arthur."

Elissa looked down at the small girl and smiled at how well she took care of herself. She knew her limits.

"Let's go," Elissa agreed without hesitation. "See ya later, boys."

"C'mon, Merlin," Earl told the wizard, who was rapidly getting wiser by the minute. "Let's go play."

Several hours later, Joslin entered the small cottage and found Wayne telling Arthur stories by the fire. The young boy jumped up and ran to Joslin. He hugged her exuberantly, almost knocking her over.

"What a reception!" she laughed as she held him close.

She looked over at Wayne, who was watching the reunion with a twinkle in his eye.

"Have a seat," he told her. "How about some mulled cider?"

Arthur led Joslin to the hearth, where she sat down to warm herself as Wayne placed a steaming cup on a little table beside her. Then he patted her on the back before sitting down. Arthur tugged at her knee.

"Tell us about the Sea Dragons. Wayne said that you and Elissa were on a major mission," Arthur encouraged her.

Joslin gazed into Arthur's eyes and softened. She loved her newfound brother. She glanced at Wayne for encouragement. He reached for Arthur, who climbed into his lap and posed regally next to Joslin. Joslin almost laughed at Arthur's throne in Wayne's lap. She felt that she was having an audience with a king. Wayne grinned and jostled Arthur on his knee, while

Arthur smiled and kept his balance. Otherwise, he gave Joslin his full attention.

"I hear that you found a contaminated well on the Druid Isle," Wayne started.

Joslin looked up at Wayne, slightly astonishment by his knowledge of events but grateful for his understanding. "One of the bricks in the well had the eye of Horus on it."

"All the bricks have the eye of Horus on them," Wayne retorted.

Arthur cocked his head from side to side to catch Wayne's point. The man's sense of humor had suddenly diminished.

Joslin caught his point and stared at the fire. She felt dazed. "We didn't have much time to investigate. Earl and Merlin are neutralizing the contaminated crystal at the cave. Elissa and I will be going back to finish checking the place out."

"Check out the other bricks," Wayne instructed. "Then get a bird's-eye view of the well itself."

Joslin blinked and nodded. "Whoever made the well contaminated the water supply."

"Plus, there's a wormhole," Wayne added.

"You mean this well has another opening."

"Try ancient Egypt." Wayne laughed gently as he resumed bouncing young Arthur in the air.

"Sounds like Elissa and I will be leaving sometime tomorrow," Joslin remarked. "I think I'll get ready for bed now."

"Queen Eilene drowned," Arthur murmured as he watched Joslin leave the hearth.

Joslin immediately turned on her heel and looked at Wayne for an explanation.

"That's how we know that the well is a wormhole and has another opening somewhere else," Wayne said softly to Joslin.

A knock at the door interrupted their strained conversation.

Wayne sighed heavily and lowered Arthur to the floor. Then he rose to answer the knock on the heavy oak door. Wayne chuckled as he opened the door wide for the visitor to enter.

"Well, c'mon in," Wayne greeted the newcomer heartily. "It's about time you showed up. We were just getting ready to talk about you."

Merlin stepped inside and removed the hood that was shielding his blonde head of hair. He grinned at Wayne's greeting without responding. His eyes quickly surveyed the room, brightening when he recognized the children.

"Taking a break from the Sea Dragon's den?" He smiled at Joslin after he noticed the cheerful, warm surroundings.

"Yes," Joslin answered, delighted to see another familiar face outside of the cave, which fostered a more businesslike atmosphere.

Merlin noticed the tears welling inside Joslin's eyes and weighed the shortness of her response. Next he glanced at the small boy, who was silently eyeing him curiously. Kneeling slightly to adjust his height to Joslin's eye level, he began, "Queen Eilene had a difficult life in many ways. She was vulnerable to the frequencies of the Serpentine Federation as a result of past trauma. She had an easy transition, though we will all miss her. Eilene was one of the last links to your parents and Camelon. Gamaliel is ill, but he will survive the assault on his brain. The rest of us appear to have some kind of immunity, unlike those on the Druid Isle," he pondered as he straightened to his full height.

Then he faced Wayne, who had just finished securing the huge oak door.

"Horus' eye relates to a time wrinkle. It is the technique that they used to capture the knights of Camelon. Eilene fell under its effect again. Time regressed to ancient Egypt. The Galactic Wars occurred during that era and those who built the well want to revive an old occult group. We've got to close the door on it through the well on the Druid Isle."

"When do we leave?" Joslin asked.

"Elissa will come for us after lunch," Merlin answered. "Don't let me stop you from getting a good night's rest."

"C'mon, Arthur, you heard the man," Joslin responded as she scooped up her little brother and carried him to his bed next to hers.

Wayne retrieved some extra bedding from a nearby shelf and placed it in front of Merlin. The burgeoning wizard took the hint and arranged a spot by the hearth. Soon everyone in the cozy hut was sleeping peacefully.

The following morning, Merlin and Joslin waved good-bye to Arthur. Wayne had left early in the morning to attend to chores. Minerva had just returned from her journey to the neighboring village. She took over the care of young Arthur after the others had departed.

Merlin flew on one of the new fluorescent Sea Dragons that accompanied Elissa on the mission. As they neared the Druid Isle, a heavy mist rose from the lake and enveloped them. They landed near the contaminated well. Joslin immediately jumped off Elissa to examine the bricks on the well.

"Wayne was right. The shape of the well from the sky resembles the same design on all the bricks," Joslin commented as she scraped the moss off several bricks. "They had been planning for a long time."

"OK, Fossy, with your dragon skin so bright, you get to lead the dive through the well," Elissa encouraged.

Suddenly, Joslin understood why Elissa had chosen to bring Fossy, the lemon-yellow fluorescent Sea Dragon. The dragon's scales were also phosphorescent and illumined the dreary dark well like a druid tree at solstice. They went down the well and followed a water tunnel to another well in another part of the world. Merlin peered over the rim of the well's opening. They were in a remote desert oasis.

"Egyptian pyramids are only three hundred miles away," he whispered to the others below him in the well. "This place brings back past life memories."

"Well, don't reminisce too long," Elissa chided. "My memories of ancient Egypt are not so fond, especially after the Serpentine Federation fled to the desert and began recruiting more malcontents. If it is not the Tree of Knowledge, then it is a burning bush that comes complete with calcified rules."

"The place is vacant except for a few stragglers in that temple over there. They just seem to be milling around the place. Oops," Merlin added as he quickly ducked his head so that he would not be seen. "It is a nest for the Serpentine Federation."

"How do you know?" Elissa questioned.

"They have crowns of cobras on their ugly reptilian heads," Merlin answered. "The temple has the eye of Horus on it."

"Well, that's a dead giveaway," Elissa observed. "Let's get out of here before WE are dead."

The group swam back to the Druid Isle. They hurried out of the well and caught their breath.

"We've got to seal it," Merlin insisted.

"If we seal it on our end with a reflective surface, they won't catch on that it is a dead end," Elissa offered. "Any Serpentine that views his or her own reflection disappears into thin air because there is no soul to hold the reflection, which is another reason why they don't like water. Too many reflections from the water. They won't be doing much swimming, but they can sense the vibrations from our end and gather information."

"Got it," Merlin replied. "I'll seal it with their own bricks. That should give them a taste of their own random, senseless acts of violence."

With the help of the Sea Dragons, Joslin and Merlin tore down the old well. They used the bricks to create a seal with the eye of Horus design turned towards the inside of the well. After they had packed the last brick, Gamaliel emerged from the misty understory around them.

"Need some help?" he asked politely.

"Well, you awoke from your comatose nap just in time," Merlin dryly greeted him. "The hard work is done."

"That's good. Then I'll be heading back for a rest in the shade with my feet up." Gamaliel wryly grinned as he began to turn and walk away.

"Great to see you back in good form," Elissa interrupted.

"It is nice to be in any form," Gamaliel slowly nodded. "I hear that we lost our queen."

"Yeah, well, Time Lines don't help," said Merlin, who recalled his own brush with death. Then he continued, "We put a plug on it, though."

"Good," Gamaliel replied. "Let's keep it that way. It will be awhile before the rest of the Druid Isle recovers from the shock."

"It helped not to put all our Dragon eggs in one nest," Elissa commented.

"I see," Gamaliel answered. "No pun intended, considering we have been dealing with the eye in the sky again." Then he faced Elissa and offered, "There's another angle to pursue. Remember Lancelot's success with doing the inverse on the eye in the sky."

"Yes, Lancelot became his own little eye in the sky," Elissa recalled. "They were afraid of him because they could see right through him."

"We gotta get back to a more uncomplicated life," Gamaliel said with a nod. "KISS: keep it simple."

"Because it is complicated enough," Joslin sighed.

Chapter Nine

All it takes is a lie
To poison everything

Tune Reference: *Skyhigh*

----Jigsaw

JOSLIN FLEW ELISSA back to the Sea Dragon cave. For the moment, the tensions between the Druid Isle and Sea Dragon cave were diminished. Joslin wondered how Arthur was getting along back at Wayne's hut.

They landed softly on the floor of the sea cave. Eegan ran to meet them. He was his child-self again and carried a cloth bag containing the crown jewels.

"Now that we have the crown, the queen is gone," Elissa sighed.

"What are we going to do with them?" Eegan asked.

"Hang on to them for the moment," Elissa answered. "The stone in the crown came from King Gawain's stolen ring. The Turks will be looking for it. Dadgon becomes king of the druid network, which includes Wales where Wayne lives. If the crown jewels are ever noticed in his kingdom, then it will fuel further attacks from the Pendragon's armies. Arthur will be safe for the moment," Elissa remarked. Her caretaker quickly began cleaning the brine off her golden scales as she spoke.

"We'll keep them in the kitchen of the Sea Dragon cave," Eegan decided before he headed off for the busiest corner of the cave with the crown jewels jingling at his side. "I'll put them by the hotcakes. They will always be under watch there. I've got to get back to the high mountains of Tibet and check on the opening to the MidEarth. I want to be sure that the Serpentines have not made any inroads there."

Elissa smiled at the thought of the British crown jewels on display in her kitchen. Joslin stared wide-eyed at Eegan's departure. Events continued to move quickly.

Dadgon emerged from the hidden recesses of the sea cave and addressed Elissa. "I am heading back tomorrow. I had a dream about my sister Miriah last night. She was locked in the contaminated well. Now she has taken on guardianship, and she tells me that it is safe to return to the Druid Isle now and assume leadership."

Joslin glanced at Dadgon's tear-streaked face and offered him a gentle hug. He firmly patted her on the back before releasing her. A golden tear fell from the corner of Elissa's eye, and the Sea Dragon caught it in her palm. The tear crystalized immediately on contact with the Sea Dragon's skin. She placed the crystallized tear in Dadgon's hand and softly closed his fingers around it.

"Keep in touch," she said deliberately. "You are ready for your new role. Your sister will help you."

Dadgon kissed the golden Sea Dragon on the forehead and turned towards Earl, who waited nearby. Earl wiggled his mustache at Elissa and Joslin. "Don't forget to send us party invitations for Yuletide."

Dadgon brightened at his remark as he mounted the garnet Sea Dragon. "What do you mean? Party is at my place now! C'mon, Earl, we've got work to do. Gotta get the place in shape."

Earl turned towards Joslin and Elissa as he sighed wryly and flapped his angelic wings. Joslin and Elissa looked at each for a few seconds after Dadgon's departure. Neither knew what to expect next. Fortunately, Fossy approached them with an inspiring idea.

"It is about time you meet your fourteen-year-old half-sister, Miriah," Fossy told Joslin. "How about a night flight to a secret oasis in Egypt? I'm sure Miriah will provide protective cover. She already has the locals paying homage to her at the well. They leave her food and all kinds of wonderful things. She won't have to cook for several months. She told me so in a dream I had last night."

"Let's give Miriah another month to establish herself with the local slaves of the Serpentines," Elissa answered. "Meanwhile, Joslin can rest at Wayne's and play with Arthur. We'll slip Arthur back in as the new heir as soon as the Pendragon dies. He'll show up out of nowhere complete with the crown jewels so there won't be any doubt of his claim to the British throne."

"Miriah says that they have a special name for her," Fossy added. "They call her Mirage. "That is just how she appears to them," Fossy explained. "Miriah excelled at appearing out of nowhere. She played a lot of practical jokes on those poor druids. That's how she got sealed in the well. She would hide and then reveal herself later. It is her karma to be guardian of the well. She took these games too far. It also enables her to protect the Druid Isle from those who killed her mother. She was hiding in a pocket off the main tunnel when the well was sealed. She knew what you were doing but made no attempts to make her presence known."

"We could always send a Sea Dragon to retrieve her," Merlin interrupted when he joined the gathering.

"But she doesn't want to be rescued," Fossy insisted. "There are some new Sea Dragon cocoons in the well. She is caring for them right underneath the nose of the Serpentines, who have colonized the oasis."

"It should be interesting to see fire-breathing Sea Dragons fly out of a well in the oasis," Merlin speculated. "What a light show! That will impress those slaves who believe that the well is haunted. It is an attack on the Serpentines waiting to happen. The new Sea Dragons can practice melting those little golden cobra crowns."

"Yeah, well," Joslin sighed, changing the subject, "sounds like we should visit the oasis when the Sea Dragons are mature enough to provide smoke cover."

"Wise idea," Elissa remarked. "We'll check on them in three weeks and determine whether they are ready for us." Then Elissa also changed the subject and addressed Merlin. "What brings you here?"

"I wanted to let you know that Arthur's day has come," Merlin said. "I learned in the Marlboro village that the Turks never recovered from the last attack. The Pendragon died yesterday from battle wounds."

"Arcas's children are being called into further responsibilities," Elissa said as she began pacing the floor of the sea cave. Her caretaker hustled to keep up with her steps as he continued to groom her. "Arthur becomes king of Britain. Dadgon becomes king of the Druid Isle, Wales, and the others. The enslaved Visigoths in Egypt have made Miriah their queen. The Serpentines captured Arcas's relations in Germany and brought them back under the shadow of the pyramids."

"Let the survivors know that Pendragon's heir is alive and well," Elissa instructed. Tell them that he has been safely placed into the custody of the greatest wizard of all time. We promise Arthur will assume reign when he matures."

"That should keep them happy," Merlin remarked. "I suppose that I am the one who takes the heat for his upbringing or lack thereof."

"Ah, don't worry. Nobody will blame you after everything that you've been through," Elissa conjectured. "Mutant product of merpeople…Near-drowning by Serpentine interference…Self-cocooning…Rebirth with Sea Dragons…There's a start for you!"

Joslin laughed. She liked the idea of being able to spend time with her newfound younger brother. "Arthur can continue to stay with Wayne. I'll peek in on him for you."

"I get it. My job is to cut through the legalities," Merlin said as he rolled his eyes. "The Britons can go back to their tribal kingdoms for the time being."

"Which most have already done," Elissa added. "C'mon, Joslin, let's get you back to cottage life. I'll come for you when it is time for a respectful visit to your half-sister, who clearly is doing well on her own project."

Elissa returned Joslin to Wayne's cottage, where she waited for five months. On a crisp autumn day, she met the Sea Dragon queen in the meadow. After minimal greetings, they flew toward Egypt. When they got close to the desert oasis, a thick vapor emerged from the ground below them and hid them in a mist. Elissa landed two feet away from the well that they had previously discovered. A wispy figure stood nearby and greeted them.

"Ah, at long last, my sister," Miriah announced as she lightly walked towards Joslin and gave her a gentle embrace.

Joslin returned her hug. "I hear that you've been in hiding."

Miriah smiled at the youngster's sense of humor and the way she took charge. "Oh, I've found my calling." She looked around in the mist before adding, "There are some cute boys here."

Joslin laughed softly and peered wide-eyed through the mist. Elissa interrupted the girl-talk and got down to business, "It isn't just the new Sea Dragons making all the steam."

"I've been hot. The traitor, who built the well, accidentally fell in and drowned. Couldn't do a thing for him. He had been inspecting his work on a regular basis."

Elissa nodded. "The aliens duped him like Moses."

"And he died under Mosaic Law," Miriah answered. "As Lance discovered with his modified eye-for-an-eye technique, eventually Lance became like an eye in the sky."

"Lance took it to another level," Joslin, who was listening carefully, surmised.

"I wished that we had figured it out during the intergalactic wars of Egypt," Elissa remarked. "The Serpentines captured the seed civilizations and enslaved them. The mixed progeny became pharaohs. They kept the genetic lines pure so that the offspring would not deviate from the Serpentine agenda. Ramses II reverted and rebelled. He could have used Moses's help, but the Serpentines got to him first. They played on his bitterness and negativity, whereas Ramses just simply played."

Joslin and Miriah giggled quietly. Elissa sighed, remembering the erotic temple parties of Ramses II. Then she turned and looked at the girls. "He had a heart four times the size of Moses's. It matched his virility. By the time the Serpentines realized that they had overdone a good thing, it was too late. Even though they made off with the first born, Moses and his reptilian cohorts never made a dent in Egyptian history."

"Here, sister, this is for you," Miriah said, handing a magical staff to Joslin. "You're the designated healer in this project. I lifted it from the Serpentine temple. I thought that you could use it."

"Why thanks, Miriah, you're so thoughtful," Joslin replied. "Just what I always needed, a link to the temple groupies that turned Ramses's heart as well as his head."

"Most powerful medicine around," Miriah responded. "It opens doors, especially with the Noris in the east."

"We'll take it on our next expedition," Elissa said, nodding. "Those who immigrated east had a bitter pill to swallow. They call themselves Arabs now, but they will recognize the staff and welcome you. They know you come to heal."

"Sounds like you have Egypt covered," Joslin observed.

"I get by with a little help from my friends," Miriah acknowledged as she shared a parcel of food that had been left by the well as an offering. "It is getting close to daylight, and you must leave before the Serpentines discover you. Thank you, Elissa, for your training in deep-water breathing. I've put it to good use. Joslin, keep in touch."

Miriah disappeared as the mists became denser. Joslin and Elissa recognized their moment to leave the oasis without being seen. Elissa flapped her wings and emitted a breath of fire for show. Then they soared high above the oasis and returned to the sea cave to debrief the others.

Chapter Ten

Instincts bring clarity

And burn facades

Tune Reference: *In Your Eyes*

----Peter Gabriel

ELISSA FLEW BACK to the meadow near Wayne's cottage in Wales. She knew that Joslin needed time to rest after visiting her half-sister in Egypt. When they landed, Joslin affectionately kissed the golden Sea Dragon on her scaly, gold cheek and waved her off. Then she walked toward Wayne's cottage, which was about a quarter of a mile away. The sun was setting quickly, casting a golden hue over the fading horizon.

Wayne, who had been watching the skies overhead, opened the door widely for Joslin to enter.

"C'mon in and have a seat," he said delightedly. "Minerva made some soup. Have a bowl while it is still warm. Arthur is off playing with the rest of the children in the village. He'll be coming home soon."

Joslin sat down at the table as Wayne placed a piping hot bowl of homemade soup in front of her. She realized that she was very exhausted from her excursion and was grateful to be back, enjoying Wayne's hospitality.

"How's Miriah?" he asked as he sat down near her.

"She's doing all right playing with those people in Egypt. Don't tell anyone, but I think she is having fun over there. She has developed a fondness for some of the young men who have suddenly taken up the chore of collecting water. She is going to upset the gender role-playing there, much to the dismay of the Serpentines, who don't seem to know what hit them."

"Sounds good, sounds good," Wayne chuckled. "Glad to hear that she is having a fun time with it all."

"Yeah, me too," Joslin replied, and she quickly ate her soup. "Looks like I'll be heading for Arabia next."

"How about checking on Assyria? Take that staff with you," he said, nodding to the metal rod that Joslin had left at the door.

"What is so important about bringing the staff?" Joslin questioned.

"That's how you communicate with the Thunder People," he replied. "Just put it in the ground and don't touch it."

Joslin attempted to follow his thoughts. "The lighting will touch the metal rod with its replies," she surmised.

"Yes, it will also protect you from any stray streaks," Wayne replied as he rose and carried off her bowl to clean it.

Several months later, Joslin said good-bye to Arthur, Minerva, and Wayne. She hurried over to the meadow and met Elissa.

"Off to Assyria today," she said to Elissa to confirm her understanding of last night's dream.

Elissa nodded without a word. The Sea Dragon noticed that Joslin held the metal staff in her hand and smiled her acknowledgment. She felt the girl tighten her grip on the reins and flapped her angelic wings for lift. As they neared Assyria, Joslin voiced her thoughts.

"Wayne said to look for the Noris. They were a seed civilization asked to keep balance on Earth after the Serpentines destroyed their planet."

Elissa landed in front of a stone palace with statue of a Sea Dragon at the entrance. Joslin dismounted and climbed the stairs toward the statue.

"She's got your eyes," Joslin remarked as she lightly caressed the statue.

"That's my mother," Elissa commented. "She helped with the refugees fleeing Atlantis. Her name was Ea. I see her during eclipses. She inhabits the celestial realm now."

"Does anyone live in the palace now?" Joslin asked, surveying her surroundings. "It seems vacant."

"King Ormuz is on his way," Elissa answered. "He is hiding in another dimension, and it will take a moment for us to find each other. We've got to find the right combination of energies. It has been a thousand years since anyone contacted this civilization. The mechanisms are a little rusty."

Joslin pondered the Sea Dragon queen's words for a moment. Then she asked, "Why is King Ormuz in hiding?"

"There is a huge Serpentine outpost in the mountains north of us. They created a powerful three-headed dragon who is half-human. It was one of their few surviving experiments. Fortunately, it has never been able to reproduce, but no one has been able to kill it either."

"Glad I asked," Joslin replied as she uneasily studied the northern mountains of Armenia. She noticed a red hue in the skies over Armenia, as if fires were burning on the mountaintops. A shiver ran up Joslin's spine. Then she heard a rumble of thunder coming from the southeast. There were lighting streaks darting across the southeastern sky.

"The Thunder People are coming," Elissa told her. "They are telling us that we are in danger."

"Oh," Joslin said. She noticed that the northern skies were becoming redder. "I think that it is time to put in my stake."

Joslin stuck the metal rod in a crevice between two steps on the palace stairs. A sudden gust of wind blew sand around the pole and it swirled around the statue of Ea. With every heavy gust, the lightning moved nearer, until finally a bolt found its way to the metal rod. When lightning struck the staff, the skies suddenly darkened and raindrops began to pelt the stone steps, leaving small indentations in the hardened sand. King Ormuz and his constituents appeared in the darkness. Torchlights from within the palace walls illumined the structure and the many faces of those who lived there.

"Over here," King Ormuz greeted Joslin. "Come, let's get out of the rain while the Thunder People speak."

"We are looking for the Noris," explained Elissa, who did not want to stay any longer than necessary in another dimension.

"I know," King Ormuz replied, "but we still need to make contact," he said with a happy wink at Joslin.

King Ormuz led them to a cozy room with a roaring fire at the far end and a round table made of white stone. Small piles of food and drink were scattered across the table. Merlin and a white-eared Sea Dragon were already seated and munching on purple grapes.

"Merlin, how did you get here so fast?" Elissa asked. "When you didn't show up as scheduled at the sea cave, I left without you."

"I was coaching some ogres on Roman retaliation," Merlin replied. "I tried to get a message across the waveguide at Stonehenge, but it was jammed. So I flew Fossy to Miriah's well. I had heard that the new white-eared Sea Dragons at the well are fairly savvy at intradimensional flights. They can travel within the same dimension without getting sidetracked. Miriah wanted to show a florescent dragon at the well for a few days, so we traded. It is only for a few days. Anyways, the experimental intradimensional test flight turned out well. Here we are. Just in time for the light show."

A subsequent roll of thunder and several lightning streaks emphasized Merlin's words. Joslin studied the sky outside the small window opposite the fire. She saw a red haze in the distance making its way to the palace. Joslin silently poked Elissa and discretely pointed to the great ball of fire. Elissa gasped.

"I think we have a rupture in the intradimensional bubble. A wildfire is heading our way," Elissa interrupted. "About those Noris?"

"The same thing happened to them," King Ormuz remarked. "Great balls of fire! Most went to China where they could balance the elements better. Look up Fa Hien; he can help you find the rest at the Valley of the Indus. They call themselves Hindoos and seek a more internal sort of balance called Vedic. We need to grid it into the Stonehenge network. They've had proven success with it."

"Time to go," Merlin announced. "King Ormuz, I hate to eat and run …Thank you for your hospitality…Until we meet again," he said with a generous bow before turning towards Elissa. "Meet me in Socotra! It is the middle of monsoon season there."

"That's a quick way to balance the elements," King Ormuz observed. Then he turned to an aide who had already retrieved Joslin's metal staff. King Ormuz thanked the aide for his thoughtfulness and returned Joslin's staff to her.

"Notice that the metal rod is hollow," he instructed her. "I crafted this for your father when we were small boys on the Druid Isle. It served as a prototype for the structures we added to the Avebury site."

Joslin nodded and mounted Elissa on the adjacent veranda. She shook the staff proudly in the air and smiled at King Ormuz. King Ormuz waved as the mighty Sea Dragon queen lifted into the air.

"Until we meet again," he yelled as he disappeared in a swirling gust of wind.

Joslin and Elissa watched the palace disappear in the desert sandstorm. Seconds later the great ball of fire reached the area below them. Finding nothing to consume, the fire leaped high into the air and singed the edge of Elissa's golden tail. The Sea Dragon winced in pain and propelled herself farther into the darkening skies overhead.

Moments later they landed in a rainstorm on a gray beach. Elissa gently lowered Joslin to the ground so that she could inspect the wound. Merlin and his White-eared Sea Dragon rushed out from underneath a palm tree to meet them.

"So happy to see that you were able to track us in all that confusion," he shouted above the thundering raindrops. Then he spotted the wound on Elissa's tail. "You're bleeding!"

A drop of blood fell on the beach. A tiny plant suddenly emerged from the site where the Sea Dragon's blood spilled. Joslin applied compression to stop the bleeding while watching the seedling take shape.

"We'll call it Dragon's Blood Tree," she yelled. Then she nodded to Elissa, "Let's go find a cave and build our own fire."

Chapter Eleven

There's no time

For fooling around

During a war

That's how you know

You are in one

Tune Reference: *Life During Wartime*

----Talking Heads

The next morning, the group of Dragon flyers and Sea Dragons flew to China. Rather than land on the mainland, they opted for an island that the traders from the Ports of Gaul (Portugal by 700AD) called Formosa. Merlin and Joslin hid the Sea Dragons in the forest before approaching the townspeople on foot. Many of the inhabitants had fled the mainland after the fall of the Han dynasty. A few hundred yards outside of town, a Chinese monk stepped out of the shadows.

"I am Fa Hien, the one you seek," he told them. "I saw you and your dragons in the sky. Can I have a lift to India?"

"Yes, and you can help us find the eastern Noris," Merlin replied.

"I am Han Chinese. The Han are refugees from the Milky Way. We could use a few pointers from the Noris, who are masters of outer space travel as well as inner space. The Noris figured out a way to get past the Serpentine Federation. Their Vedic system of balance complements our Buddhist-Taoist-Confucian mix. I need to know more."

"Great, and we need to know where they ran off," Joslin added.

"Let's go grab the Sea Dragons and leave for the desert beyond the Great Wall. We'll use our interdimensional techniques to elude the Serpentines and their monsters."

Joslin led the way back to the Sea Dragons, where Merlin hoisted Fa Hien on the back of the white-eared Sea Dragon.

"What is her name?" Fa Hien asked.

"Cleo," the shiny yellow, White-eared Sea Dragon said in a silky voice.

"Got it," Fa Hien said as Merlin strapped him to the Sea Dragon's back.

Then Merlin hopped on Cleo's back, and she spread her angelic wings and joined the others, who were already high in the sky. After a brief rest at a city near the Great Wall, they crossed the Gobi Desert to join a party in Khotan, an oasis known for its lavish celebrations. The inhabitants had learned of the travelers through meditative dreams underneath grapevines. Having literally heard the news through the grapevine, the Buddhists expressed sheer delight in seeing their dreams come true. They shared their gems, spices, silks, and wine with the weary travelers. Then they left the next day for an oasis in Afghanistan, where they caught up with the wandering Eastern Noris.

"Long last, no see," Merlin said to the head monk at the temple.

"I see." The monk bowed with a cocky grin. "I give you two minutes before the Serpentines chase you out with their Great Balls of Fire."

"In that case, where can we go for safety?" Merlin inquired with a bow.

"Down the mountains of the Hindu Kush," the monk answered. Then he briefly interrupted his bow with a mild jerk. "And watch your tush."

"Point taken," Merlin dryly replied. "OK, gang," he addressed his friends. "Save your tush by sliding down the Kush. Tally-ho!"

They hurried out of Afghanistan and descended into a valley at the base of the mountains. Great Balls of Fire loomed in the skies behind them. The Indus River flowed from the snowmelt in the high mountains. They followed the course of the Indus to the lower valley. For some mysterious reason, the three-headed dragon ceased its pursuit at the beginning of the Indus River.

"Obviously, Great Balls of Fire doesn't like to get his feet wet," Merlin remarked as they watched Great Balls of Fire stop on the nearby mountaintop.

"Well, he gets steamed," Joslin observed, watching Great Balls of Fire disappear in his own vapor.

"Now is our big chance to escape while he can't see," Elissa encouraged.

"I agree," Merlin said as he hurried toward an outlying village in the valley. "Trouble always comes in threes. Great Balls of Fire lends new meaning to the term dragon breath."

Elissa tossed her golden head in response. "I get by with a little bit of help from my caretaker. Nobody can get close to that beast."

"Poor misunderstood Serpentine monster," Merlin added in mock sympathy. "Somebody dropped a figure in his system of checks and balances."

"Can we get on with the flight?" Joslin asked, exasperated. "Look, there are some Hindoos looking at us. Let's land there."

Merlin sighed and sped his White-eared Sea Dragon toward the crowd developing on the banks of the Indus River.

"Thank you so much for steaming Great Balls of Fire!" the Hindoo disciples greeted them. "We could use a little more rain."

"Surely you could find a better way," Charles, the other White-eared Sea Dragon, quipped. He had remained quiet during most of the travels so far. Charles was known for being a patient Sea Dragon, which is why Merlin chose to bring him instead of the others.

"What's up, Charles?" Merlin asked. He knew better than to ignore an irked Sea Dragon, especially when it was Charles.

"Well, my brother Ferndale has a special knack for rainmaking. He has a way of harmonizing with the seasonal rains to increase the fertility of the oasis," Charles replied. "The oasis owes its stability to him."

"Can we get him here?" one of the disciples inquired. Then she added, "What can we do to attract him?"

"Wait a minute here," Joslin, who excelled in math, interrupted. "You really need three Sea Dragons to balance Great Balls of Fire. One for each head."

"She has a point," Elissa nodded. "The issue may be a little more complicated. We narrowly escaped with two dragons. Three dragons should really keep him steamed."

"That should keep Great Balls of Fire out of the weather!" Merlin joked with a touch of sarcasm. He was beginning to understand Charles's point.

"I was thinking that the sight of the three Sea Dragons would serve to neutralize Great Balls of Fire's effect while Ferndale plays rainmaker," Joslin continued.

Merlin quieted for a moment before replying, "Hmm, that might work. It is a little tricky, but Great Balls of Fire isn't known for his brains."

"It is worth a try," Elissa answered. "In exchange, the Hindoos can impart some of their Vedic knowledge on balance to the Sea Dragons and Fa Hien. There will be no sacred cows here unless they are used to provide cream for Ferndale's breakfast. He is fond of cream, you know."

Fa Hien, who had been silent during most of the discussion, remained silent and eagerly nodded. The Hindoos were impressed by his lack of words and eagerly agreed to the deal. They immediately began assisting the visitors with Dragon care and refreshments.

"We'll send Ferndale, the maroon and gold dragon with white ears," Merlin continued, thinking out loud. "Mighty Moe, his bright red sibling, will want to come. Mighty Moe is very protective of his smaller brother, Ferndale. They will want to bring Sissy, their bigger, older sister, along. Sissy is a huge blue-green Sea Dragon with white ears. Her color matches the color of the Indus River, and it will confound Great Balls of Fire even more. Although she is a relatively large Sea Dragon, Sissy prefers running to fighting. She could probably make the headwaters of the Indus River in two seconds. This will make Great Balls of Fire steam that much faster and the mountains will get snow. Ferndale can take it over from there."

"Great, that matches our system of balances very well," one of the Hindoo disciples acknowledged. "We have essentially three doshas or elements to consider. The first is vata, which is air. The second is pitta, which is fire. The third element, kapha, refers to the planet and represents a mixture of both earth and water. By balancing these three doshas, we can make an oasis out of the desert."

"Got it," Fa Hien said, making points by keeping communication simple.

A young female disciple moved forward and walked with Merlin as they led him and the others to the heart of the village.

"What kind of structure shall we build for the Sea Dragons?" she asked.

"Oh, a nice stone residence. Preferably with a view of the water," Merlin replied absentmindedly. "A temple structure will do. They like open air and they come complete with their own caretakers and Dragon flyers. So you'll need a place for the humans too. Sea Dragons almost get treated like gods and goddesses, you know."

Elissa overheard Merlin's last remark and bopped the wizard on his posterior with her golden, scaly tail.

"Well, you see, Sea Dragons are very busy creatures. They simply don't have time for such important details," Merlin corrected himself before he eyed Elissa. Then he moved out of the way of her tail before adding, "I should know because I was raised by Sea Dragons. They are like Mum and Pop to me."

Joslin sighed as Merlin hurried into the village and out of Elissa's reach. She turned to the disciples and smiled at them diplomatically. "Don't mind him. He still behaves like a very mischievous boy. Then again, somebody has to keep those Sea Dragons on their toes."

The disciples giggled. They left Joslin to chase Merlin. Later, the Hindoos succeeded in drafting him to help refurbish their temple for the prospective four Sea Dragons.

Chapter Twelve

Good vibrations

Of playful color and light

Create a whole new world

Tune Reference: *Good Vibrations*

----The Beach Boys

A FEW MONTHS later, Joslin returned to Wayne's cottage while Merlin stayed behind to help prepare a place for the remaining three Sea Dragons. Joslin kissed Elissa affectionately on the check and waved her off. She began walking through the meadow toward Wayne's cottage on the other side of the adjacent forest. Snow had fallen, and she had missed the seasonal transition from autumn to winter. This time she didn't feel as if she had missed anything. Somehow she had managed to keep the pulse of the countryside and hearth within her. She felt herself slipping into the rhythm of Wales as if she had never really left it. Gazing into the distance, she noticed a small figure bobbing over the uneven terrain of the snowy meadows. Joslin smiled when she recognized her younger brother, Arthur.

"I saw your Sea Dragon in the sky," he explained as he almost toppled her with a hug.

"I missed you," Joslin answered as she lifted Arthur with a gentle embrace.

"Minerva just made some fresh soup this morning," he told her with a slight bounce in his step. "We are happy you will be able to join us for dinner."

Joslin laughed and hurried after Arthur, who quickly led the way through the icy trails back home. She could tell that he had spent some time exploring the wintry habitat. Arthur seemed to know every bump in the road. Joslin was grateful that she had not needed to rediscover it on her own. She might not have recognized the path.

When they reached the heavy oak door of the cottage, Joslin stopped briefly with a sigh. "Thank you for showing me the way," she said as she softly squeezed his small hand.

He looked up at her with a smile and then confidently opened the door for her as he excitedly pushed her inside.

"Joslin's back!" he yelled happily.

Wayne chuckled and rose to usher Joslin to a seat by the hearth where Minerva sat knitting a sweater. Minerva kissed Joslin on the cheek when Joslin went over to embrace her. After hugging Wayne, she assumed her place by the fire. Arthur quickly sat down beside her.

"How goes it with those Sea Dragons?" Wayne asked as he handed Joslin a cup of warm cider. "I hear that you went to old Arabia."

"That was one of the places. Then we made our way through China to India."

"Did you find the Hindoos?" he quizzed her.

"Oh yes, and we lent them three Sea Dragons," she continued. "They are needed to ward off Great Balls of Fire and keep their valley fertile."

"Great Balls of Fire!" Arthur echoed, lifting his head.

Wayne studied the boy's excitement and chuckled again.

"It is a three-headed loser from the Serpentines' experimentation," Joslin explained.

"Is it very ferocious?" Arthur questioned.

"Just hot and stupid," Joslin answered. "We like to keep it hot and bothered. No one can get close enough to put it out of its misery."

"Sounds like you will need to learn how to take the heat," Minerva observed. "It is something every queen should know."

Arthur giggled, rubbing his tiny hands together in delight. He had been part of Wayne and Minerva's discussion concerning Joslin's future.

"I suppose you are right," Joslin replied. "Great Balls of Fire is the least of my fears."

"You are ready for the next step in Sea Dragon training," Minerva remarked.

"I can use all the help I can get," Joslin observed. "I don't want to repeat Queen Eilene's mistakes."

"The Sea Dragons can help you there," Wayne responded. "They have an exercise called Nine Dragons where they impart some of their gifts to you. It empowers as well as elevates the practitioner."

"Sounds good," Joslin said. "When do we start?"

"You have been building up to it already," Wayne commented. "I'll talk to Elissa and Earl, and we will set it up for a hundred days from today. We were discussing it shortly after finding out that Queen Eilene had drowned."

A hundred days later, Joslin met nine Sea Dragons in their cave by the sea. Earl and Elissa, the first Sea Dragons to cocoon, decided to serve as Joslin's guardians. The other seven Sea Dragons represented the four types of batches that had occurred in the Sea Dragon history. The first batch included the one that Joslin had witnessed. It marked the beginning of the Sea Dragons' campaign after the Furry Dragons retreated to MidEarth. Her grandmother's Furry Dragon represented the second type from MidEarth. The third type pertained to the psychedelic Sea Dragons lost in the Caribbean. The fourth type consisted of the fluorescent Sea Dragons.

"By facing your worst nightmare, you will gain the gift of seership and vision," Elissa explained. "Just stand in the middle of the circle."

"I always hated to be the middle of attention," Joslin admitted.

"We know," Earl confessed. "There will only be seven Sea Dragons encircling you. Elissa and I will stand outside the circle, posted on the north and south directions."

Joslin stood in the middle of the circle of seven Sea Dragons as Earl and Elissa took their posts. For the moment, most of the Sea Dragons ignored Joslin and busied themselves with last-minute preparations. Joslin watched Earl twirl his mustache while Marebell, a blue dragon, shined a large fingernail. Her grandmother's Furry Dragon was fluffing up her fur like a cat on a hot wire. Paisley, the psychedelic Sea Dragon, played deafening twangs on a string instrument that he had fashioned from the hair of a tiger. One of the fluorescent Sea Dragons practiced shadow boxing on the wall of the cave.

"How long do we go for?" Joslin inquired of Elissa.

"Until they scare you to death," Earl replied.

"Oh, well that shouldn't take long," Joslin admitted.

"You are tougher than you think," Elissa said. "Let's get going. OK, Sea Dragons, on the count of three, I want to see your best scare. No slackers. One, two, three..."

At the count of three, all the Sea Dragons in the circle breathed on Joslin. Although none of the flames touched her, they came close. They screamed and flapped their mighty wings at her. Joslin watched the commotion from the center of the circle with wide eyes.

"That's it. Be fierce Sea Dragons. Make sure she feels the heat," Elissa encouraged.

Almost an hour later, Earl called the Sea Dragons off. "I think we got it."

Joslin emerged from the center a changed person. Her hair and eyes had changed. Her auburn hair now had a deep, dark-red hue. Her brown eyes had turned blue and gained a piercing quality and a cornea cover like a cat's.

"Good job," Earl remarked, twirling his mustache in delight. "How do you feel, Joslin?"

"Changed," she remarked.

"What scared you the most?" Earl questioned her.

"I began to fear that I might miss lunch," she said. "Can I go back to Wales now?"

"Aye, the lunch bit works every time," Earl wistfully replied.

"Let's get you back home," Elissa responded. "You did well today, and you've got the hairstyle to show it."

Wayne was up waiting for Joslin when she arrived at the cottage. Minerva had taken Arthur to visit with friends in a nearby village. They had stayed overnight to spread the lengthy journey over two days.

"I see you passed," Wayne said as he poured a bowl of soup for her. Then he carried it over to where Joslin sat staring at the fire. "The first exercise pertained to the cultivation of sight and knowingness. Tell me about the different batches of Sea Dragons."

"The first group offered the gift of seeing as awareness. They were the first to cocoon in response to the call," Joslin began slowly. "The second batch included my grandmother's Furry Dragon and gave me the gift of sight as wisdom and the ability to see through the ages. The third batch consisted of the psychedelic Sea Dragons, who had been lost since the collapse of Atlantis. Somehow they eluded the Serpentines and survived. They gave me the sense of vision, which is needed for thriving instead of just surviving."

Joslin blinked hard as spoke, and Wayne nodded for her to continue.

"The fourth group presented me with the gift of self-illumination and being able to see my way through darkness. They were the fluorescent Sea Dragons that glow in the dark."

Joslin finished and began to eat her soup while Wayne thought about her words. Then he added, "There are two more exercises."

"I had a feeling that there were more. The White-eared Sea Dragons from Miriah's Egyptian well were missing."

"There is another batch of Sea Dragons cocooning now," Wayne continued. "You helped stir things up. More are being called to action."

Joslin stared at Wayne as he spoke. "Where are these cocooning?" she questioned him.

"Merlin found them in the Caspian Sea. I ran into him today. He is back from his adventures with the Hindoos," Wayne told her. "He wanted me to give you this amulet from the Hindoos."

Joslin accepted the blue, white, and yellow pendant. "It looks like an eye."

"It is," Wayne answered. "The Turks call it Nazar. It is carried for protection from the 'evil eye.'"

Joslin rubbed the flat pendant in her hands and curiously examined it. "You mean they have had similar close encounters with the eye in the sky or eye of Horus?"

"It's a small world," Wayne said with an air of mystery. "The various seed civilizations have their own methods for protection. Some work better than others."

"I see," Joslin said as she gazed into the fire again.

"We all do now," Wayne added as he sat down in his chair beside her.

Almost a year later, Joslin returned to the sea cave for the second exercise. This time there were twelve Sea Dragons, including two new types. Joslin noticed two White-eared Sea Dragons from Egypt. Another new Sea Dragon came from the batch that had cocooned at the Caspian Sea. He sported a Nazar at the tip of every one of his silver scales. Called Hawkeye, he shimmered in the moonlight. A second new Sea Dragon came from the China Sea. This brilliant red Sea Dragon had jade gemstones at the tips of her scales and ears. Fa Hien and Merlin had found these hatchlings after bringing the white-eared Sea Dragons to the Indus River.

"Ready for a head trip?" Earl quizzed as Joslin centered herself amongst eight Sea Dragons.

Elissa shot Earl a blazing glance in reprimand. Then she turned toward Joslin with a loud correction, "Exercise two is the gift of travel through magic."

"Magic!" Earl shot back. Then he offered Joslin another correction. "It is called relativity, my dear. It is a specialty in physics."

Elissa ignored Earl's correction and continued. "This time you have Sea Dragon guardians at all four corners outside the circle. East, west, north, and south."

"Humph," Earl said. "Let's get going. My turn to count. At the count of three, Sea Dragons, move it!"

When the Sea Dragons heard the countdown, they began swooping and flying over Joslin's head. They kept the same scare tactics as earlier. They moved around and darted at her for almost an hour. Suddenly she became so dizzy that she vomited.

"Good job!" Earl announced. "I say, you've done it!"

The Sea Dragons stopped and went back to their caretakers for more grooming. Joslin left the mess in the center and lay down on the floor of the sea cave. She stared at the ceiling for several minutes while Earl came over to check on her.

"So what did it this time?" he inquired.

"I just started remembering that there was no place like home. No place like home…" Joslin replied.

"Home is where the heart is!" Earl jubilantly paraphrased. "There goes the fluid in the middle ear. Bye-bye, balance. Hello, nausea!"

"Can I go back to the cottage?" Joslin asked in a feeble voice.

Moments later Joslin recounted to Arthur and Wayne the details of exercise two, otherwise known as Twelve Dragons.

"What a trip!" she told them in an animated voice. "The Sea Dragons with the jade ears and white ears were travelers of inner space. They offered the gift of intradimensional travel."

Arthur smiled delightedly and tried to imagine the appearance of the red Sea Dragon with jade ears. Wayne smiled and gazed softly at the fire.

"The Sea Dragon with the Nazars on his silver scales imparted the knowledge of outer space travel. He knew the motions of the universe in astrological as wells as astronomical terms. What a dragon! Whew!"

"I bet that the Nazars keep him safe during his travels so that he can move undetected," Arthur reasoned.

"You know, I think you're right," Joslin replied, pondering over the possibilities.

"That's good. You are getting it," Wayne encouraged. He rose from his chair to refill his mug. "Now you are ready to visit the hatchlings in Africa, South America, and Thailand."

"Oh," Joslin said, thinking it over. "Let me guess, the third and final set is called Fifteen Dragons."

Chapter Thirteen

Northern towns

Die quickly

Tune Reference: *Life In A Northern Town*

----Dream Academy

WAYNE WAVED JOSLIN off early the next morning. She still felt groggy from the exercises the day before, but a good night's sleep and hearty breakfast helped considerably. Elissa met her at the meadow.

"How are you doing?" the golden Sea Dragon queen asked her as Joslin shimmied up her back.

"I'm here," Joslin answered. "And I'm ready to go."

"Ninety percent of it is just showing up," Elissa said as she flapped her giant, angelic wings.

"Where are we going today?" Joslin thought to ask after they had reached altitude.

"Someplace you've never been before," Elissa replied.

"All the places have been like that," Joslin reminded her.

"Oh," murmured Elissa, recalling the past itineraries. Then she shook her head to correct her memory. "Well, we are going to Africa."

Moments later Elissa landed at the edge of Kalambo Falls. Joslin dismounted and examined some of the ancient writings on a nearby stone wall. At a small lake behind the falls, she noticed some stone tools left in disarray.

"Those were left by a seed star civilization that the sea serpents carried to safety during the Great Cataclysm," Elissa commented. "The Great Cataclysm sunk Atlantis."

"Where are they now?" Joslin questioned.

"They ascended when their civilization was attacked by the Serpentines," Elissa answered. "The Serpentines had already contaminated their DNA, and their abilities degenerated as a result. In the end their features became cruder, and they had to resort to basic hand tools for survival."

Joslin wiped a tear from her cheek as she turned and headed for the refreshing view of the falls. Elissa looked around at the area that had once boasted a thriving human population. Then she followed Joslin to the edge of the cliff.

"Where are the hatchlings?" Joslin inquired as she watched water spill over the cliff into the valley below.

"They are coming. I can sense their presence," Elissa answered. "It takes a while for a large Sea Dragon to maneuver through the jungle underbrush undetected."

Seconds later several large Sea Dragons wiggled out of the understory. Each scale on their sleek bodies had a diamond embedded on the tip. Compared to the other dragons, they were much larger for their level of maturation.

"Very good," Elissa remarked to the tropical-colored Sea Dragons around her. "I see that you have kept your spit and polish despite the circumstances."

"Ah, all it takes to make a diamond from coal is a little heat and pressure," Glitter, the shiniest Sea Dragon next to Elissa, offered. Glitter lightly kissed her older sister on the cheek and continued, "Besides, diamonds are a girl's best friend."

"You could probably cut through glass with a little power behind those rocks," Joslin remarked, wiping a fern fragment off the scale closest to her.

"If we don't blind them by the light first," added Shiny, the tiniest Sea Dragon of the lot.

"Well-done," Elissa praised, surveying the group around her.

"Tell us about it," sighed Sawtooth, the roughest Sea Dragon of them all. "We were all just diamonds in the rough."

"Say no more," Elissa interrupted. "It is party time now! Speaking of which, where are the others?"

"Well, we sorta got lost and separated over the years of wear and tear," Shiny admitted. "With so much sparkle, we lost focus. But it is never too late for a party. Some of the others are divided amongst six waterfalls of the Zambezi River. First there is the Lumange Waterfall, and then there are Ntumbachushi. Mumbuluma, Kabweluma, Chisimba, and finally Mosi-oa-Tunya, which really smokes when it thunders."

"Other Sea Dragons cocooned at Lake Tanganyika. During a heavy rain, the lake spilled over into the Congo River. Some of the sea serpents went on to shoot the rapids of that river and opted for saltwater at the Congo Estuary. This gave them easy access to the Atlantic Ocean, which has a small fish in a big pond feel to it."

"We have our upstream Sea Dragons and our downstream Sea Dragons," Elissa observed. "Not to mention those who prefer freshwater to saltwater. No bother. The party is at Lake Tanganyika, where the African Sea Dragon started out. Be there or be square."

"The jungle will never be the same again!" Shiny said. "Meet you there in three hours." Then he addressed the others, "C'mon, we've got a feast to put on."

The other Sea Dragons quickly scurried away into the underbrush and disappeared in seconds. Joslin and Elissa headed straight for Lake Tanganyika. Many of the Sea Dragons that joined them had brightly colored permanent headdresses. The feathers adorned their faces like a crown or colorful sunset, setting off their diamond scales in a multitude of hues.

"Care to dance?" a tropical-colored Sea Dragon named Abu asked Joslin.

"I'm next!" Tucan, another colorful and feathered Sea Dragon, quipped.

Joslin smiled and stepped in time to the jungle drumbeat with the others.

"How about a line dance?" she diplomatically offered.

Elissa nudged the Sea Dragons into a line and danced behind them. More Sea Dragons followed them in step. Soon there was a row of colorful, dancing Sea Dragons snaking its way along the banks of Lake Tanganyika.

"Oh! We should have done this sooner," Abu remarked. "I am out of rhythm."

"Practice makes perfect," Elissa encouraged as she happily swirled around. "Every night to the jungle beat."

"What if the Serpentines detect us?" Tucan questioned.

"I doubt anyone would want to come close to this crowd," Elissa said.

Tucan studied the diamond-studded group. "You have a point. We have given new meaning to the term cutting the rug."

"Party on," Elissa continued. "Dance the night away, if not the darkness."

"We can dance until dawn!" Abu enthusiastically shouted.

After the sixth set, Joslin retired for the night, but most of the Sea Dragons kept dancing. Elissa joined her shortly afterward.

"Don't want to overdo a good thing," Elissa observed as she curled up next to Joslin underneath a tree. "Next week we fly to the jungles of South America."

"OK," Joslin said half-asleep. The steady drumbeat lulled her like a heartbeat. She quickly fell into a deep slumber.

The next week she and Elissa waved good-bye to the African Sea Dragons and flew across the Atlantic to South America. They landed at the headwaters of the Amazon River and met more Sea Dragons that sported tropical colors. The Sea Dragons from Peru had emeralds embedded in the tips of their scales. Some of the Sea Dragons also had feathered headdresses, but the feathers were similar to the regional birds like macaws and parrots rather than the ostriches and cranes.

"How are you?" Fabu asked. This fabulous emerald-studded Sea Dragon came adorned with green macaw feathers crowning his head.

The collection of South American Sea Dragons appeared very regal with scepters and stately bows. In comparison the African Sea Dragons seemed more soulful with clear, bright eyes that both soothed and pierced the hearts of those around them. Joslin watched the South American Sea Dragons puff their chests with pride. She could see their mighty hearts pumping beneath their muscular chests, and it reminded her of the rhythm of the jungle.

"Would you like some chocolate?" offered Gabriella, a divinely ornate Sea Dragon with blue feathers and emeralds. "You must come with us to the pyramids of Peru."

Joslin curiously glanced at Elissa. She was not aware that there were other pyramids in the world besides those in Egypt. Elissa met the girl's gaze and then responded to Gabriella's invitation.

"We'd love to see the old Sea Dragon base from the intergalactic wars!" Elissa exclaimed with heartfelt enthusiasm. "Let's bring some of that fantastic chocolate."

Moments later Joslin soared high in the sky with a royal band of Sea Dragons. They landed on the flat top of a pyramid. Joslin dismounted and surveyed the vast steps leading down the structure.

"Every step counts," Elissa commented, noting her interest. "The structure was designed to harmonize with fundamental frequencies of the galaxy. It creates a heartfelt connection."

"It appears relatively peaceful," Joslin commented as she investigated some of the interior rooms.

"This one was never invaded by the Serpentine Federation, but they seized operation of the ones farther north before abandoning them. The Serpentines made the captives worship them as gods and impregnated the seed civilizations. Those who had pure blood had their hearts removed and died."

"Why the hearts?" Joslin questioned, running her fingers over a design on the walls of a corridor.

"They thought that by taking the hearts of their victims, they might gain a sense of compassion," Elissa replied, shaking her head. "In reality it was a senseless act of violence. The Serpentines are too jaded to be very bright."

"I'd like to visit the northern pyramids," Joslin announced as she emerged from a corridor into the daylight.

"OK, let's go to Teotihuacán," Elissa told the other Sea Dragons in their group.

They made their way into the heart of present-day Mexico and landed on the tops of pyramids scattered around the area. The natives hurried to care for the Sea Dragons and greet Joslin. The City of Pyramids was almost as big as Camelon during the height of activity.

"So this is where they take care of the Sea Dragons who fight the Serpentine Federation in North America," Joslin remarked as the natives ushered her down a flight of stairs and inside a corridor in the pyramid.

"Yes," Elissa replied. "There are several Sea Dragon bases there. They are concerned about being attacked here, but so far they have managed to elude the Serpentines."

"That is why we don't waste time on the tops of the pyramids," added Juan, one of the natives who had met her earlier. "Come meet the Sea Dragon under my care. His name is Taco."

"I'm Taco," a proud Sea Dragon waiting for them inside the corridor piped.

Although he was tropical red, Taco lacked the gemstones of African and South American Sea Dragons. His head was covered with a fine headdress of purple macaw feathers.

"So happy to see you all," he said with an elegant bow. "We heard that you were on tour."

A native served them a chocolate drink and mixed fruit in a side dish. Joslin studied the murals in the room. Her eyes centered on a stone circle at the end of the corridor. She recognized it as a calendar.

"I had a bet with Taco that you would find that calendar right away," said Amiga, a brightly colored Sea Dragon of tropical blue colors and a green-feathered headdress. She turned and poked the Sea Dragon next to her in the ribs. "OK, Taco, that will be thirty-four bars of chocolate."

Taco winced. "You win. Let's explain the calendar first before I dig out my stash in my lair."

Amiga smiled confidently and began talking about the calendar. "One of the Mayan refugees brought it here. It had been in the temple at Machu Picchu, where it had been gridded with the Stonehenge network."

"When we hid Machu Picchu in another dimension, we put the reemergence date on the calendar," Taco continued.

Joslin studied the calendar. "Do you mean 2012?"

"No, that's when the calendar resets itself," Taco said. "Reemergence comes after the reset, which is 2013."

"So what happens with the 2012 reset?" Joslin asked.

"The experiment with the Serpentine Federation is over," Amiga and Taco chimed in unison. "We put an ending on the deal and gridded it into another dimension."

"Do you think we will have everything moved into the other dimension by then?" Joslin asked.

"I hope," Taco sighed with a rather sad shake of his regal feathers.

"There's still plenty of time," Elissa interjected.

"Congratulations!" Joslin brightened, shaking the hands of those around her. Some hands were scaled; some were skin. None were fur in this part of the world. Then she added, "This generation's gift to the Stonehenge network will be compassion, especially for oneself. Thank you so much for your insight and direction on this project."

Elissa beamed. It was a great day in history.

Chapter Fourteen

Sometimes you can overdo

A good thing

Tune Reference: *Great Balls Of Fire*

----Jerry Lee Lewis

A WEEK LATER Elissa returned Joslin to the meadow. She waved off the golden Sea Dragon queen before spotting her younger brother heading through the late-summer grasses and flowers. He ran toward her with a bouquet of freshly picked wildflowers.

"Here," he said exuberantly. "These are for you. I hear that you had a birthday last week."

"The Sea Dragons in Mexico threw a party for my ten-year birthday," Joslin replied as she accepted the wildflowers. After examining the arrangement, she lightly inhaled the aroma for a brief moment. Then she smiled and peered down at Arthur. Joslin lifted him to her in a gentle embrace. "Thank you."

Arthur smiled and gave a little hop after she lowered him to the ground. He took her by the hand and led her to Wayne and Minerva's cottage. When they arrived at the cottage, he opened the door and gently guided her inside.

"How was Mexico?" Wayne asked as he ushered her to a place by the hearth.

Joslin stopped by Minerva, who was knitting by the fire, and tenderly embraced her without disrupting her needlework. Minerva kissed her and patted Joslin gently on the shoulder. Joslin sat down in a chair beside her. Arthur brought her a cup of tea with a bowl of thick soup.

"We have a present for you," Wayne announced. He produced a shining dress of armor from the coat rack near the fireplace mantle. The armor flowed in the air like a dress but had wide-legged pants for dragon flying and warmth. The fabric was weaved from millions of tiny diamonds that reflected the surroundings almost like a mirror. Whoever wore the dress of armor blended into the surroundings and appeared invisible, unless they moved in contrast to the background.

Joslin gasped. She was astonished at the beautiful yet practical garment. She leaped to her feet and went over to admire the armor. She noticed that the material weighed very little.

"Put it on," Wayne urged. "Those African dragons have been working overtime."

Joslin slipped the armor over her clothes. Arthur rubbed his tiny hands together in delight; the armor's reflection of the fire was almost blinding. She felt awestruck by the sight of her hands and forearms disappearing in the light.

Minerva dropped her knitting and stood to help Joslin arrange the armor for different purposes. Joslin learned how to wear the armor for camouflage or for blinding opponents.

"Be careful with those," Wayne commented after Joslin nearly sawed an arm off the chair where she had been sitting.

"Bring your arms down like a cloud so that the diamonds in your material don't slice the furniture," Minerva instructed Joslin.

Arthur giggled.

Wayne shrugged and grinned slyly. "Practice makes perfect."

Joslin practiced a few more cloud sets before giving it up in the late afternoon. She carefully removed the outer garment and hung it on the cloak rack. Then she stood a few steps away from the armor and examined every fold and crease.

"It is almost time for the third ritual," Joslin softly acknowledged while admiring the armor's breastplate. It was a magician's breastplate, made out of amber, which provided psychic protection. Rubies and sapphires adorned the breastplate at specific points in the amber design. The gems shielded the wearer of the armor from aberrant frequencies. She felt a little nervous about the third exercise. The appearance of the armor hinted subtly at the gravity of the situation. A shudder ran up her spine.

"Yes, you have a month to practice with the armor. It will prepare you for the third set," Wayne said in almost a whisper.

Joslin nodded and studied the design on the breastplate closely. She intended to become familiar with the armor as if it was her best friend. She would learn how to master the power that it contained.

A month later Joslin joined thirty-five Sea Dragons in the sea cave. Thirty-one Sea Dragons encircled her with four Sea Dragons posted at east, west, north, and south positions. Representative Sea Dragons from Africa, South America, and Mexico came to join the circle. When Earl gave the count, all the Sea Dragons in the circle did their best to scare Joslin.

After forty minutes had elapsed, the third exercise was interrupted by a loud screech at the entrance of the cave. Seconds later a giant flame entered the cave and stopped a foot short of the Sea Dragon stationed at the west post. All the Sea Dragons paused briefly to identify the cause of the threatening flame.

"It's Great Balls Of Fire!" the Furry Dragon that had belonged to Joslin's grandmother shouted. She had been stationed at the west post, and her fur had barely missed catching on fire.

Immediately, two Sea Dragons from Africa left the circle and flew into the flames. They disappeared completely as they pursued the source of the fire. A shrill scream pierced the smoky air. It trailed off in agony for several seconds before being silenced. When the smoke finally cleared, the severed torso of Great Balls of Fire lay on the floor of the cave. The African Sea Dragons had used their sharp, diamond-studded forearms to cut the three-headed beast in half.

"Dinnertime for the sharks," Earl announced as he lifted half of the beast and headed for the waves outside the cave. "Nothing is ever wasted."

One of the White-eared Sea Dragons removed the rest of the body and followed Earl. The Furry Dragon that had belonged to Joslin's grandmother approached the trembling girl who had been forgotten in the crowd of Sea Dragons. The crowd quieted to hear what the Furry Dragon had to say. Elissa silently remained at her post on the north, while Puff stood still at his position on the east post. Joslin ran to her grandmother's Furry Dragon and buried her face in the soft white fur. The Furry Dragon noticed a huge tear was falling from the exposed side of Joslin's cheek. She looked down at the wet fur underneath the girl's face. Then she cuddled the child in her soft arms.

"It's over," the Furry Dragon said. "Great Balls of Fire is out of his misery. Sauron's experiment in post-Atlantean genetics can no longer inflict his suffering on the world."

Joslin shook her head and buried it farther in the dragon's furry abdomen. Elissa vacated her post and waved the other Sea Dragons off. Some offered a few good-byes, but most just quietly left with a smile and nod.

"Your thoughts resonated with Great Balls of Fire, and he tracked you here. Somehow you were able to get inside his programming," Elissa explained when she joined the Furry Dragon at Joslin's side. "You did what nobody, not even the Serpentines, could do."

Joslin nodded her head without moving from the comfort of the Furry Dragon. "With everything I've seen in the world lately, I found myself feeling sorry for myself."

Elissa glanced at the Furry Dragon with a knowing smile. She compassionately stroked the girl's shoulder.

"There's a place for that," the golden Sea Dragon queen remarked. "Let it out. You are long overdue for a good cry."

Joslin continued to sob until she fell asleep in the arms of her grandmother's Furry Dragon. She spent a quiet night in the warm cave. The next day, Elissa returned her to the meadow near Wayne and Minerva's cottage. Joslin slid off the back of the Sea Dragon and slowly walked to the cottage. It was dusk, and darkness had settled by the time she entered the familiar room that she called home. She was surprised to find the room empty but with a roaring fire in the hearth.

"SURPRISE!" a chorus of voices sang.

Wayne, Minerva, and Arthur stepped out from their hiding places and embraced Joslin. In the dimly lit room, Joslin could see fairies dancing in the air, leaving phosphorescent swirls of dust behind them. A leprechaun perched on the windowsill lit a candle that illuminated the room. Several elves and gnomes emerged from the darkness.

"Congratulations!" they told her as Wayne beamed. "Thanks for taking care of Great Balls of Fire so that we could safely exit the MidEarth through the cave in Tibet."

"Like Great Balls of Fire, they also heard your call," Wayne explained. "The MidEarth inhabitants are at your service."

Joslin blinked wide-eyed at the gnomes. She had heard that they all died out before Gamaliel even met his adopted parent.

"We found out that not all gnomes became sterile as a result of the Serpentine experiments," commented a fairy fluttering at Joslin's shoulder. "There's a thriving community now in the MidEarth."

They celebrated for over two hours and then left for encampments in the nearby forests. Wayne and Minerva tucked Joslin and Arthur into bed. A sense of peace descended on the cottage, and Joslin felt relaxed for the first time in a long while. She and Arthur quickly fell into a restful asleep.

Chapter Fifteen

Just keep singing

Until you go

And keep dreaming

Until something comes through

For you

Tune Reference: *Dream On*

----Aerosmith

A FAIRY WEARING a pink dress appeared at the end of Joslin's bed when she awoke the next morning. She fluttered her silvery wings when Joslin noticed her. She resembled the fairy that Joslin had dreamed about last night, except she looked different in the daylight. Now she was less of a dream, more a reality. Joslin rose from the bed and the fairy flittered away. Out of the corner of her eye, Joslin saw the fairy disappear through a keyhole in the door. She changed her clothes silently so that she did not disturb young Arthur, who slept soundly in the alcove. Moments later the heavy oak door opened and Wayne walked into the room carrying a bundle of wood. After quietly placing the wood on the pile near the hearth, he addressed Joslin with a light chuckle. "The pink fairy told me that you were up," he said as he glanced around the room to see if there were any more. Then he laughed softly so that he didn't awake Arthur. "Don't let those fairies run your life.

They make themselves so tiny that they easily fit into everyone's business. On the other hand, you'll never be short for company."

Joslin handed Wayne a cup of hot cider and motioned him to a chair at the table. Then she leaned toward him, almost whispering, "This one got into my dreams last night."

Wayne leaned back and chuckled. "Oh they do that. They will help you stay on track. What did she want you to know?"

"She told me that the Serpentines will be preoccupied with the Byzantine Empire for the next thousand years. The best tactic is to deal with Grays on the North American continent and secure freedom in that region. It would give the advantage in dealing with the Serpentines later. By the time Constantinople falls, people will be looking toward the West for answers." Then Joslin leaned back in reflection. "It would be helpful if the West was able to provide those answers."

Wayne grinned slightly, staring into the steam coming off his hot mug. "When do you head back to Mexico?"

"I'll go back to the training base in a few months," Joslin answered, looking into the steam rising from Wayne's mug. "I want to get to know this community from the MidEarth. They are refugees from the temperate and Arctic zones. That was the time when Furry Dragons were preferred to Sea Dragons in this type of warfare. Sea Dragons can handle the tropics easier than the Furry Dragons."

Wayne eyed Joslin as he added, "The Gray's base is in the Great Lakes region. Sea Dragons suit that area very well. A few already have established underwater caves there." Then he winked, "Now there's some advantageous footing for you. Slippery when wet, but you know all about that."

Joslin rubbed her scaled fingers together and laughed silently. A sparkle came to her eyes, almost as sparkly as the wings of the pink fairy that had visited her dreams. "After the Grays leave, we can move out some of the MidEarth refugees to North America."

"There's a plan," he said, teasingly slapping her thigh. "Now get outside and play. I'll send out your brother when he gets ready."

Joslin looked at her Arthur, who remained sleeping peacefully. She finished breakfast and then went outside to meet the MidEarth community. Leprechauns, elves, gnomes, and fairies made ideal playmates. Not only were they wise, but they were also very versatile. They showed her other worlds of flora and fauna that she never knew existed. She learned that if she could dream it, then she could do it. They taught her how to use her imagination as a problem-solving tool. At first the MidEarth communities really stretched her imagination, but she adapted by opening herself to the magic of possibilities, which weaved dreams into realities.

Two months later Elissa met Joslin in the meadow. "Now I am the one being summoned instead of doing the summoning," Elissa remarked as Joslin climbed on her back with her metal rod. This time she wore her armor and appeared invisible to any casual observer. Her armor matched the golden color of the Sea Dragon queen perfectly, and Joslin knew how to move with the dragon to remain undetected even through unexpected motions.

"We must visit Miriah," Joslin told her. "I dreamed that she had some information for me. She knows that we are coming."

Without a further word, Elissa took off for the skies over Egypt. She felt pleased that Joslin had stepped into a leadership position and had taken control over the challenges facing the Dragon flyers. When they were over the Egyptian oasis, a great mist enveloped their bodies, shielding them from view while they landed a few feet from the well.

"I discovered the identity of the traitor who built the well that killed my mother," Miriah said, getting straight to the point after she quickly embraced her half-sister.

Joslin stepped back to brace herself for the emotional shock. Elissa glanced at Joslin and nodded her understanding of the importance of the matter. Joslin patted Elissa's cheek affectionately as Miriah continued.

"It was your great-grandfather's great-great-great nephew. The one they named after King Cole. The Romans knew him as King Colius II. He would have been your fourth cousin."

"That fits," Elissa commented. "King Cole escaped from England and regrouped in Scotland. Camelon was named for Camulodunum, which is the region that his family had occupied before Roman colonization. His great-great grandmother, Brodica, had tried to regain her kingdom but failed. King Cole's daughter, Athildis, was a consort to Marcomir IV, king of the Salien Franks. Both Tristan and Lancelot were Marcomir's grandsons. When internal conflicts rose within the family concerning the practice of dark occultism, Athildis fled and found refuge with King Beli's family in Rome. Beli married Anna, the niece of Joseph of Arimathea. Later Athildis married one of their sons, Afallach. Afallach's older brother, John the Baptist, heralded a rebellion of the Israelites against Rome. Athildis's grandson was named for her brother, King Cole. The Romans made him a puppet king of the colony at Camulodunum and named him Colius II. Colius II renamed the colony and called it Colchester. He built this well and cut a deal with the Serpentines. His reign became short-lived. His daughter, Helena of Colchester, became consort to the Roman Emperor Constantius and gave birth to Constantine. With her help Constantine became emperor of Rome. His forces attacked those that had regrouped at Camelon. King Pellinor, one of her relations, picked up where she left off."

Joslin steadied herself at Elissa's side. Ever since the intergalactic wars of ancient Egypt, the Serpentines had been mixing with seed civilizations and then destroying those who did not fulfill their agenda. Like a snake, they sometimes ate their own young. Their infiltration into native genetic lines had devastating results on harmony within families. The families and communities tended to self-destruct as a result.

"Where do we go from here?" Joslin questioned. Then she added, "Can you prove that this well was made by King Colius II? We need to be certain."

"Yes, I can," Miriah answered. "I simply looked it up in the archives of the Druid Isle. Gamaliel commissioned him to make this well."

Elissa gave a little puff at this revelation.

"Gamaliel failed to mention this when we closed the contaminated well," Joslin observed. "We suspected that he and your mother were forming alliances with the Romans at their base in Londinium."

"I know," Miriah admitted. "So did I. That is why I hid in the well and conducted my own investigations. Gamaliel confessed and showed me the archives after the effects of the contamination wore off. I confronted him on a hunch."

Joslin sighed. "I dreamed that there was a connection between this well and the Castle Marlboro."

Miriah nodded before continuing, "I also uncovered it during my investigations. They used it to infiltrate the Castle Marlboro. Erin, my blue white-eared Sea Dragon, is guarding the other end. She will provide cover vapor when you visit the ruins."

"How did you guess that was my next stop?" Joslin smiled as she turned and quickly mounted Elissa.

Joslin's warm, direct acknowledgment replaced a parting embrace, which would seem awkward given the seriousness of the subject. There was no further discussion or need for thanks. Miriah waved as the fog began to reappear from the well and cloak it in obscurity. The golden Sea Dragon queen lifted her great, angelic wings and took off into the surrounding mists. The ruins of the Castle Marlboro were the last place on Earth that Joslin personally wanted to revisit. She wiped a tear from her eye as she recalled the airlift during the Roman invasion. Queen Maury's daughter, Nimue, had done her best to defend the castle after it had been restored. The Romans captured and tortured the queen to death with multiple rapes and mutilations. Fortunately, they had managed to rescue the queen's son, Gareth, and save him from spiritual annihilation. Since the death of her father and Camelon knights, the Romans had perfected the technique of obliterating a soul with unimaginable psychological violations. Though she felt comforted by the knowledge that white-eared Sea Dragons had driven the Romans away, she was afraid of discovering painful associations relating to her own past.

Elissa gracefully landed in the middle of the vapor emerging from the nearby river and castle ruins. Joslin dismounted and searched for the secret passageway that she recalled from her visit six years ago. She located the well in the center of the courtyard. Then she turned around, surveying the fallen walls for a hint of a faded memory. The mist around the courtyard began to dissipate while the vapor formed a protective bubble around the castle ruins. As Joslin searched the area for familiar places, a shiny, blue white-eared Sea Dragon emerged from the well. Elissa gestured for Joslin to turn around and see the rising Sea Dragon.

"It's great to meet you, Erin," Elissa greeted her as Joslin regained her composure at the sight of the Sea Dragon.

"Oh, my friends," Erin answered in a sweet voice. "It is so nice to see you. Please make yourselves comfortable. I'll have my caretaker, Evan, bring refreshments."

"Must be great to have a break from chasing Romans," Elissa commented as Evan appeared with fortified dragon grog and a cup of cider for Joslin.

"Yes, it seems that the meaner they are, the faster they run," Erin answered. "Roman soldiers are so cowardly."

"I know," Elissa replied, sipping her dragon's grog with refinement.

Joslin relaxed and slowly drank her cider. Evan reappeared with dragon gruel and soup for Joslin. He had been spending his free time rebuilding rooms in the castle. In the distant corner of the courtyard, a ghost emerged from a small room within the fallen tower. Joslin gasped as she watched the wispy figure of Queen Nimue approach them. The soft-spoken queen stood dressed in an elaborate gown, unmarred from the hostilities that had taken her life and spirit. She went over to Erin and tenderly put her translucent, white arms around her torso.

"Welcome," Queen Nimue said, nodding towards the remaining castle. Then she added in almost an apologetic voice, "There isn't much left."

"I can see that," Elissa said as she looked over Queen Nimue. "I'll have to send Merlin here to help. He is a great survivor."

"I guess that I won't need to look for the secret passageway," Joslin observed. "I have my own guide right here."

Queen Nimue buried her head in Erin's wing and rubbed her cheek. She affectionately stoked the Sea Dragon's back as she turned toward Joslin. "I can tell you what you need to know."

"Yes, I can see that you are still taking care of the place," Joslin began, feeling uncomfortable about going in the silent castle.

"The battle is at Londinium, otherwise known as Augustus," Nimue said, redirecting Joslin's focus. "The sun god temple serves as headquarters for Serpentine Federation. The Grays operate the temple for the Federation while they are busy in Constantinople. The Grail worshippers sent King Lud, son of King Beli, to govern the Roman colony. His mother was the niece of Joseph of Arimathea. Beli's mother was the daughter of Emperor Tiberus, who made Joseph of Arimathea a decorated Roman noble. Joseph was a metals trader and supplied the Roman soldiers with their armaments. Joseph's nephew Simon was the real king of the Israelites, rather than Jesse, the mutated merman whom they crucified with the other rebels. The Romans killed Simon when they sacked Jerusalem forty years later, then they joined the Grail worshipers and resurrected Jesse as their leader."

"I think my father mentioned that Joseph of Arimathea had put enough lead in the Romans' water supply to make them all crazy," Joslin recalled.

"They like their blood," Queen Nimue insisted, thoughtfully rubbing the site where the Roman soldiers had inflicted a facial wound. Despite the fleeting memory, her translucent skin remained unscarred.

"I get it," Joslin said. "Attack London, level the Temple of Mithras, and sever Briton from Rome as well as Constantine."

"That would be a start," Queen Nimue answered.

"Great. We'll do it next month during Beltane, which is on May first," Joslin decided. "Beltane is a Roman party named after the governor, who was only a quarter Celtic. We'll show them a party. The druids can help us."

"Once a Trojan horse, always a Trojan horse," Elissa observed. "Crash the Roman Grail worshippers' party. Restore harmony to the people descended from King Brute of Troy."

Chapter Sixteen

When I mask myself
I can't be fooled

Tune Reference: *I Wear My Sunglasses At Night*
----Corey Hart

WELL," JOSLIN SAID as she turned toward the golden Sea Dragon queen. Joslin motioned to Elissa that she was ready to leave the Castle Marlboro. She nodded to the ghost of Queen Nimue before mounting the golden Sea Dragon queen. "Merlin can help you with the soul retrieval. We have no time to spare. I need the help of celestials to seize London. Time to pay a visit to the surviving Angles in Germany."

"Your great-grandmother was an Angle," Elissa remarked.

"Ingrod often sought refuge at the royal castle there until the Serpentines attacked my father's parents there. For hundreds of years, it was the safest place on earth," Joslin answered.

Elissa soared high into the air, beyond the mists that enveloped them for security. They landed in a small village on a peninsula called Angeln. Many of the villagers rushed out of their sod huts to greet them. They immediately recognized Joslin as King Arthur's daughter. The metal staff that she carried served to emphasize the relationship in their minds.

"Oh! We wondered if we would ever see the likes of your father again!" a slender, beautiful woman exclaimed. "I am the life partner of his brother, Ergan."

Joslin embraced the woman as some of her ten cousins encircled her with heartwarming smiles. Joslin turned and hugged as many of them as she could all at once. They reminded her of her father in many ways. She felt comfortable with them even though she had never met them. The wars had separated them. After Ergan died in a dragon flying raid, his children moved to the peninsula with the other fleeing members of the royal family. Ingrod chose to defend the castle from invaders as a decoy. It bought the refugees time, and they escaped safely. They remained in hiding after the fall of Marlboro and Camelon. For several years they had been growing in numbers and strength. They remained unharmed as the rest of the world fell to Constantinople.

"We switched to Sea Dragons," Joslin explained, noting the curiosity of the gathering crowd.

Elissa raised her proud, golden head, offering a puff of smoke for emphasis. The group cheered with delight and summoned some former caretakers of the Furry Dragons for help. The caretakers immediately arrived with Dragon grog for Elissa, while the others led Joslin inside one of the huts. Overnight, they planned a raid on the Roman encampment known as Londinium.

"Hit Mithras' Temple first," Joslin instructed. "I know they will call us barbarians, but the temple will make a great station for the Sea Dragons. It is roomy and has a few open-air skylights. We took a look at the place on the way here."

"We'll just move in," one of her older cousins replied. "It may take a few years, but I think persistence will pay off. We need to push the influences of Constantinople out of the area. Our remaining Turkish relations can take over from there."

"Sounds like a plan," Joslin said. "We'll start with a few minor exercises for practice while your group trains with the Sea Dragons. In three years Londinium won't know what hit it."

Three years later, Joslin and the Sea Dragon forces assembled in the forests outside of Londinium. Her cousins' descendants who inhabited the forests and partnered with the Norse people joined them. These forest-dwellers were known as Saxons. Some of the Saxons mated with the immigrant Franks, and they were known as the Jutes. The Jutes were the descendants of Arthur's aunt, Athildis, who had been a consort to the Frankish King Marcomir and some of his other royal Frankish relations. After the beheading of John the Baptist, the Frankish relations of Queen Athildis left Rome to join their relatives in Germany. The Jutes included the cousins of Tristan and Lancelot. Together these three main tribes mounted a guerilla operation against the Roman invaders over a period of several hundred years.

The Armenian prince, Varazdat, had been sent by the forces at Constantinople to infiltrate the Franks with Serpentine influences. After becoming ruler of the Franks and killing Marcomir IV, he adopted the Roman name of Pharamond. He was a distant relation of Joseph of Arimathea and continued much of the family's occult practices, eventually using it against the Romans as well. His son, Merovech, arrived as the result of a dark-arts ritual and began a dynasty that covered modern-day France. Their ambitions later included Rome, which withdrew Roman soldiers from the British Isles.

Joslin and the Anglo-Saxon forces seized the opportunity to restore harmony to Briton. The abandoned Roman outposts were easily taken over. By this time druids had infiltrated the ranks of the clergy in high places. They converted the Grail worshippers to Catholics and continued to enjoy many of their favorite druidic holidays without the complexities of dark occultism.

"Look! The Angels have come to save us!" a priest exclaimed when Joslin and the winged Sea Dragons arrived at the largest cathedral, which was located on the outskirts of Londinium. His druid parents had been slaughtered by the Romans and relatives had placed him with other druid orphans in the monastery. He recognized many of the Dragon flyers as celestials from Angeln, Germany. Instead of calling them Angles, he decided to use the word 'Angels' to disguise their true identity.

Joslin appeared from underneath her armor, which radiated in the light, making her appearance even more impressive. "Most of the place will be covered in ash by tomorrow, except Arian Catholic homes and churches. They will think it is a miracle."

"Got it," the priest replied. "It will be the topic of next Sunday's sermon."

So while the Romans were pursuing the Merovingians, the Sea Dragons torched Londinium until a layer of ash covered the former Roman capital. Joslin left the city in the hands of her Anglo cousins and their Saxon children, who allowed the druids to carry on with their spiritual practices without persecution. Once the dust had settled, Joslin waved good-bye to her Anglo cousins.

"Where are you going now?" they asked.

"Off to Scythia to visit my Saxon cousins who journeyed east," she replied. "They call themselves Goths. I have a few relatives hanging out north of Rome."

However, Joslin decided to spend a night in Khotan before heading for Scythia. She wanted to pay a return visit to the oasis on the edge of the Gobi Desert. She fondly remembered their lavish celebrations and meditative states, in which the natives used the same waveguide created by the Santa Dragons thousands of years ago.

"We saw you coming in our meditations under the grapevine," they happily told her.

"Great to hear that the grapevine is working so well," Joslin answered with a smile. "Can you send out a vibe for me?"

"Sure, what's on your mind?" they questioned her.

"The gnomes," she admitted. "I think that they decided to take matters in their own hands."

"We'll see what we can pick up during our evening meditation," they told her. Later, after evening mediation, the inhabitants of Khotan informed her, "The gnomes have been very busy. If the news makes the waveguide, it is always for the best of all."

"What do you mean busy?" she asked. In the background of her subconscious thoughts, she sensed that the gnomes had been trying to catch her attention.

"Well, you know how fond the gnomes are of the Serpentines..." one enlightened Buddhist began with a hint of irony. "Not only are they a little taller now, but they have raised an army."

"Oh, that's what is on their minds," Joslin surmised. "They came flooding out of the MidEarth through the high cave in Tibet and headed for the Goths, who they knew would recognize them."

"Ingenious," another Buddhist commented.

"Gnomes have minds of their own," Joslin remarked. "They won't let anyone get in their way, especially Roman soldiers. Looks like I just need to make sure that they are pointed in the right direction."

"Good luck," they told her with a bow when Joslin left the next morning.

Joslin headed straight for the Goths' encampment near Scythia. Several riders on horseback met her on the plain. One of the riders rode with an old priest, who dismounted quickly when Joslin removed her helmet.

"Hello, Wulfila," Joslin greeted him as she lightly steadied her grip on the priest's forearm. Wulfila had been a young associate of Patrick, the Celtic bishop who had been friends with several of the Green Knights of Camelon. Wulfila had been captured by the Romans and taken to Rome, where he escaped to the east to find security with King Arthur's relations. Joslin learned of Wulfila through her father's and Wayne's recollections. He paved the way for the Goths' entry into Rome by briefing them on the Arian controversy.

"You look so much like your father," Wulfila told her as a small tear escaped his eye. "We are ready to go to Rome, and I have taken the edge off the gnomes. They want to be known as Huns now. They pressured the Goths to invade Rome and deal with the Serpentines there."

"It is difficult to shut down someone who has been hiding in the MidEarth for hundreds of years," Joslin said.

"I know," Wulfila said ruefully. "Such spirit must be accounted for in any emerging religion, especially if it is birthed from the MidEarth."

Chapter Seventeen

Being orphaned and nameless

Is a stronger identity

Than stardom

Tune Reference: *Name*

----The Goo Goo Dolls

AFTER HELPING THE Goths and Huns with subtle technicalities pertaining to the invasion of Rome, Joslin left for Spain. "Don't forget to enlist the help of the Vandals," Joslin reminded Attila, a strapping young gnome who was experiencing a growth spurt. "You'll have to take out their Roman puppet masters first, though. Then they will be most happy to come along for the ride."

"Got it," Attila said.

"Meet me in Spain afterwards," Joslin instructed.

"That's a job for the Goths," one of her younger Gothic cousins piped. "I think I have some uncles and aunts in the Pyrenees. We'll give them a hand after we finish business here."

Attila and the young Goths reminded her of her younger brother Arthur, whom she missed very much. She knew that he was busy learning the lore of the Anglo Saxons in Britain after having recently appeared in society as the heir to the Pendragon. Once Merlin produced the crown jewels, the amalgamated Turks immediately recognized the lad as one of their own, which served as a brilliant diplomatic move. There were no other contenders for king of the British Isles.

Joslin flew to Spain and landed at a base camp in the Pyrenees Mountains. The remains of King Galahad's army had fled to these mountains to avoid further confrontation with the Grail worshippers, Merovingians, and Romans. Several mountain people emerged from hidden caves and came to greet Joslin.

"The Goths are coming," Joslin told them.

"Great, we can use someone with a reputation in Rome," one of the mountain guerilla soldiers answered. "Can you send a few Vandals our way too?"

"I'll leave that up to the Goths," Joslin quipped. "I'm sure that they will have no trouble rousing a few Vandals."

Elissa interjected a few words before the conversation solely turned to business. "The Iberians from Spain have supported the Green Knights throughout the years. They have continued to do this right underneath the noses of the Roman occupation in Spain. The Romans are convinced that the Orange Knights, which really are Spanish Knights, are Britons."

"Next they will be making a House of Orange." Joslin sighed, shaking her head at the Romanized version of history on the horizon. "While the rest of the world is busy fighting for the planet, the Greeks and Romans preoccupy themselves with rewriting history."

"This brings us back to the name of these mountains," a mountain woman said. "The Greeks named the mountains for one of Hercules' rape victims, Pyrene. A serpent arose as the result of the violation. The Celts knew the mountains as Pyre, which pertains to a funeral fire."

"Although the Serpentine Federation has been a presence here ever since the Greeks, it is weak and not very well-rooted," Joslin observed. "Like Greece and Rome, it has decayed from internal as well as external forces."

Joslin remained with the surviving armies of King Galahad for five years. It was a way of repaying the Orange Knights for all their help in protecting the British Isles. Years later the Vandals and Visigoths joined forces with the prepared Pyrenees soldiers and gained control of the country.

Her stay with the knights in the Pyrenees Mountains was interrupted by an urgent visit from her brother Arthur. He arrived on Alfred, his hot-pink Sea Dragon. Alfred gracefully landed at the base and the thirteen-year-old boy hopped down.

"Eegan is missing," he reported. Arthur had made frequent visits to his sister in the Pyrenees during the past five years, which gave him a sense of familiarity with the base. He was able to easily locate his sister and get straight to the point.

Joslin looked up from the map that she and several knights were studying. When she saw the stress in her younger brother's blue eyes, she quickly left the tent for a more private area under a grove of trees. Arthur followed her out of the tent, and he and Alfred joined her under the grove.

"How long has he been gone?" she asked quietly.

"Two days," Arthur replied. "Wayne checked with the chieftain of Eegan's village after he didn't show up at the sea cave. He was teaching a class for the younger Dragon flyers about compass directions."

"Where was he seen last?" Joslin questioned.

"He has been spending his summer vacation with Imaile in the high mountains of Tibet. There has been a malfunction with the Stonehenge communications network lately. We have been unable to contact Eegan."

A shiver ran up Joslin's spine. She had an eerie feeling about Eegan's disappearance. She sensed a relationship between the disruption in communications and the high mountains of Tibet, which were also part of the network.

"Has anyone checked on Shambala in the high mountains of Tibet?" she quizzed him.

"We are sending a group of Dragon flyers tomorrow," Arthur said. "All the ones who have been trained for Shambala were busy on missions all over the globe. This event caught us off guard."

"Tell them to hold off," Joslin commanded. "It might be a trap. What if the Grays have finally landed in Shambala? You can use the communications network here."

Minutes later Arthur returned to the grove where Joslin remained, looking out at the countryside. She had been so busy that it had been awhile since she last gazed at the spectacular view. Now she gave herself a moment to reflect.

"You're correct," Arthur told her. "The surrounding communication centers confirm that the Grays landed at Shambala and jammed the network there. Eegan escaped with the help of the Three Wise Kings through the Star Bubble."

"Where is its closest station?" Joslin asked him.

"Mongolia," Arthur answered. 'There is one other thing, though. There are some Sea Dragon cocoons there."

"Hmm, that's an interesting coincidence," Joslin observed. She took a few paces and stared into a different direction. "Elissa and I will search for Eegan in Mongolia while envoys gather information about the Grays' invasion in Shambala. Tell MidEarth to seal the cave so that the Grays do not find the entrance. We'll be shutting down Shambala, allowing the vegetation to die off. In a few months, it will look like any other arid mountaintop."

Arthur hurried off to the sea cave to oversee the envoys going to Shambala. Joslin finished her work at the base in the Pyrenees Mountains before heading to the sea cave to gather a group of Dragon flyers that would accompany her. She summoned Murphy and his Sea Dragon named Paisley; McGrail and his Sea Dragon called Gilderoy; Scott and the Sea Dragon Mansford; O'Leary and the Sea Dragon Drummond; and MacLean and the brilliant red Sea Dragon Egraine. Together they flew from the coast of Wales to the Mongolian desert.

A brilliant star shone brightly over the desert night sky. Joslin recognized it as the planet Jupiter. Shortly before the birth of Jesse, the mutated merman that Joseph of Arimathea had adopted, the Three Magi had used the star sphere connected to this planet. When it aligned with the planet Jupiter and Star Regulus, the three time travelers used the light of the alignment to travel to Joseph's home in Nazareth. Later the star sphere took them to Bethlehem where they met with some of the Anglo celestials, who were chatting with the local shepherds. Joseph and his niece Miriam had taken the infant to Bethlehem to pass him off as their own child for the Roman census.

Joslin spotted the star sphere parked in the middle of the desert and landed a few yards away from it. The star sphere reflected the surrounding images and blended into the scenery like her armor. Joslin saw through the camouflage and found Eegan trapped inside the star sphere. Eegan waved to her in acknowledgment and then motioned her away from the site. Joslin and her group of Dragon flyers backed off and hid behind some nearby boulders one hundred yards away. Minutes after their hasty departure, Joslin watched thirty Gray extraterrestrials appear beside the star sphere and rattle Eegan's bubble. They had seen through the camouflage. When they touched the star sphere, it no longer reflected the light of its surroundings and became visible. They continued trying to break the star sphere until they were joined by four newly hatched Sea Dragons with unkempt scales and bat-like wings. Then they focused their attention on the newcomers.

Joslin gasped at the sight of the traitor Sea Dragons. Their departure from the Light had caused their features to become more serpentine. Their scales were rough and had lost their shimmer. Their eyes were red and hollow. Several Dragon flyers appeared around the traitor Sea Dragons. They had bargained with the Grays and forged an alliance. These traitors were Turkish nomads who had been exiled by infighting within the Byzantine Empire. They remained militant and pursued destruction for material gain. Nothing else mattered to them, especially spiritual concerns. They tried to extract Eegan from the star sphere, but it continued to hold. Eventually they gave up and went away.

After the traitors had disappeared over the horizon, Eegan motioned for Joslin and the others to come closer. "That's quite an exercise in learning how to feel safe in your own egg," Joslin remarked as she studied the star sphere.

Eegan just smiled and nodded a little. Joslin positioned her magical staff in the sand ten feet away from the star sphere. She sensed that the staff created by King Ormuz might interact with the resonant frequency of the star sphere and pop Eegan out of the bubble. It worked. The wall that had remained impermeable to the Grays suddenly became permeable. Eegan stepped out and waved a casual greeting to everyone.

"I suppose we won't be needing those hatchlings," Joslin shrewdly commented as she hugged Eegan. "I am glad that you are safe."

"While practicing chi gung in Shambala, I found myself being transported by the star sphere," he said. After some reflection, he admitted, "I had been doing the set where you put yourself in a protective egg. While doing the Taoist exercise, I lapsed into a deep meditation and opened the Golden Flower in my mind's eye. Then I fell into the star sphere."

"And in the nick of time," Joslin added. "Your training saved you. The Grays landed in Shambala and somehow managed to track your transport. Luckily, they couldn't get to you."

Eegan sighed and dropped his shoulders. He had assumed the age that he enjoyed when he was around Joslin. In her presence, he would always be four years older, which made him twenty-four now. He explained to Joslin, "The light connection with Jupiter transported me to the exact place where the new Sea Dragons had cocooned. We needed to see what was going on here."

"The new Sea Dragons intended to cocoon at Lake Hovsgol, the beautiful dark-blue lake near the Saridag Range," Joslin continued. "They changed their minds and cocooned at the Shilka River."

"That's close to the original Serpentine lab where they conducted experiments on the children of the Arctos," Eegan commented. "The Grays operated the Serpentine lab. The traitors must have cut some sort of deal with the Grays."

Joslin and Eegan continued their discussion into the night as they made camp on the steppes. Then they waited. They knew that that Three Magi would appear once Jupiter rose in the night sky.

Chapter Eighteen

Look for that spark from within
To warm you

Tune Reference: *Firework*
----Katy Perry

SEVERAL HOURS LATER, Jupiter appeared in the eastern sky. A caravan with three kings arrived in the bright starlight through the star sphere. They easily exited the bubble and stood before Joslin and Eegan.

"We have a message for you," explained one of the Wise Kings.

Joslin recognized the group as time travelers seeded from the star Regulus, also known as the King Star in the Leo constellation. They remained as ascended masters and used the star sphere to travel through time and space. Sometimes there were as many as forty kings in the caravan. Only three kings formed the core group. There were no women accompanying the kings on their journeys because it was their role to operate the base satellite from the multiple stars comprising Regulus.

"The Grays' main base is in the Great Lakes region," Jasper said, serving as one of the kings associated with China. "The war is there rather than in Shambala or Mongolia."

"Thanks for letting us know," Joslin said.

"But there is more that you should know," Melchoir, interceded. This time traveler maintained associations with Arabia.

"Tell us," Joslin answered.

"When we followed the conjunction of our star Regulus with Jupiter and Venus, we found the hiding place of Joseph of Arimathea. He had the kidnapped infant from the merpeople with him. He had an alias as Herod Antipas, a Herodian freedom fighter from the house of Judah. At the time he was meeting with the Parthians, Rome's foremost enemy."

"The Serpentines learned of the meetings and instructed the Romans to kill his family and all infants in the area," Bathasa, interjected. This magi frequented Ethiopia.

"And what about those druid settlements that Joseph or Herod destroyed in Briton?" Joslin questioned.

"They staged it," Melchoir answered. "He destroyed the settlements before the Romans got to them and helped relocate the majority of druids to the local clergy or mountains."

"Do you expect me to believe this?" Joslin asked.

"Go back to the ghost at the Castle Marlboro," Jasper suggested. "Your father, Arcas, helped with the continuing relocations, but these decisions had been made long before his time. Not even Queen Maury knew about it. Maury was too close to her family members who collaborated with the Romans.

"We brought Herod Antipas gifts for his kingdom and encouraged him to trade with India for their quality spices such as myrrh and frankincense. He needed the gold to barter for the safety of his family. He cut a deal with the father of the child. He had been a merman. They called it a kidnapping to avoid being detected by the Serpentines, who would have killed any bargain with the merpeople. The placement of the child was their last hope against the genocide perpetrated by Morgan Le Fey."

"Herod Antipas wanted to use the child to overthrow the Romans in an insurrection," Melchoir explained when he saw the anger flashing in Joslin's eyes. "As much as the Romans seeded the Serpentine influence, Herod's plan was to counter with the seeding of light. The child was a direct descendant of a Light Being. The merpeople are considered Light Beings and evolved from the spirit that created this planet."

"Sounds like child sacrifice to me," Joslin sighed, wiping away a little tear that had fallen from her eye. She shook her head. "So they used a double for the resurrection?"

"Jesse had many brothers that were willing to fill in," Jasper remarked. "Once it is in the collective conscious of the merpeople with an alpha wave resonance, it is considered a prearranged deal. Jesse fulfilled his role well, though nobody anticipated so many traitors amongst the Herodians. The cousin of Joseph of Arimathea reported the conspiracy to the Roman royalty, who were always on the alert for any surviving earth spirit. Like Morgan Le Fey, they also viewed them as a threat to their dominion. Joseph's cousin was named for Herod the Great, the Roman general in charge of Judea who helped Joseph escape safely to Egypt. Herod the Great became a co-conspirator, though they credit him with the murders of thousands of innocents. The cousin's name was Herod Agrippa."

"I think I'll pass on the ghost at the Castle Marlboro," Joslin acquiesced. She sat down on a rock next to Eegan, who had been thoughtfully listening. Then she looked imploringly at the Three Wise Kings around her. "So this represented the divine universal plan?"

Bathasa verified, "We almost succeeded in bringing heaven to earth in one dazzling moment. Now it is a little more complicated, but at least some of the groundwork has been laid."

"I see," Joslin said. "What do you want me to do? Be explicit, please."

"Be the queen!" Jasper begged.

"Oh, so that is what all this is about," Joslin replied. "So you guys show up whenever there is a kingdom in the making."

"Got it," Bathasa answered. "Not only are we time travelers, but we serve as archetypes."

"I'll think about the archetype part later," Joslin said. "What kind of kingdom do you mean?"

"Well, the MidEarth for starts," Jasper began. "Then throw in the galaxy."

"Anything else?" she asked, rising from her position on the rock.

"Spirit of the earth?" Jasper added.

"Can I bring my little brother Arthur in on the deal?" Joslin questioned.

"We already consulted him. Being a patriarchal society, we naturally thought of him first. He passed the job to you and told us where we could find you looking for Eegan. Eegan blundered into our star sphere at the right moment."

Joslin glanced at Eegan, who merely shrugged at her. Then she threw her hands in the air. "All right, you've got your queen, but I share the job with Arthur. Let's not repeat old mistakes. My investigations have shown me that the galaxy needs to go for balance."

At that precise synchronous moment, Arthur came running through the star sphere. He spoke before Joslin could press him for further details.

"We had to destroy the sea cave before the Grays get there," Arthur announced breathlessly. "They found the hyperlink from Shambala."

"Looks like we have our king too," Bathasa observed, ignoring the bad news.

Joslin heard him but ignored the wise guy. "Where are the others?"

"Mexico," he replied. "They went to the training base there."

"Any casualties?" Joslin queried, dreading the answer.

"Nine," he admitted. "Three Sea Dragons, one caretaker, and five Dragon flyers."

"Sounds like the Grays got in pretty close. Enough to kill nine," Joslin said pointedly.

Arthur violently nodded at her with wide eyes. Then he admitted to the Three Wise Men, "See why I passed the job to my older sister."

"We can do this together," Joslin quickly told him. She hated having to hash out family politics in the midst of strangers. "This queen job scares me."

Recalling Joslin as a young trainee, Elissa spoke up. "That's why she makes a great one."

"Great!" Jasper exclaimed. "We can show you how the co-ruler model really works. There are at least thirty of us, and we all get along. Somehow it all works out, even with the women running the show at the Regulus station."

"See you in Mexico!" Melchoir waved before turning towards his camel. "As part of the deal, we'll lend you our support."

"Wonderful," Joslin said with a touch of blatant sarcasm. "That's really putting Light on the subject. What do you have in mind?"

"The Grays have never been popular in the galaxy," Jasper elaborated. He pulled Melchoir back into the group. "In fact, they stink."

"I could have told you that," Eegan quipped, wiggling his nose as he stood and eyed Joslin.

Joslin understood the meaning of Eegan's stare. She turned and confronted the group of Three Wise Kings. "Did Imaile put you up to this?"

Chapter Nineteen

Being the light in the darkness

Is no fun

It's all gray

Tune Reference: *Kiss From A Rose*

----Seal

"NO, THE IDEA came from the women at the base station," Melchoir confessed. "They felt that the planet needed a more commanding Light presence."

"Imaile waits for you at the training pyramid in Mexico," Jasper continued. Then he assured her, "We'll meet you in the starlight overlooking the snow-covered lakes. It will be winter in that part of the world."

"Fine, thanks," Joslin said as she motioned for the others to mount their Sea Dragons. At this point in history, she wasn't ready to rely on any help, no matter how well-intentioned.

The Wise Kings watched them disappear into the night without a further word. The Dragon flyers flew straight for Mexico and landed in the bright sun on the top of the Pyramid to the Moon. They quickly dismounted and hurried inside a nearby corridor. Several caretakers greeted them inside the corridor and ushered them down the hall.

"*Hola, Taco y Amiga!*" Joslin called out the greeting as she entered the room at the end of the hall. She and her group of Dragon flyers gave the brightly colored Sea Dragons a round of high fives.

"Hello, Pepe!" Eegan yelled, heartily slapping the local Dragon flyer leader on the back.

Pepe turned around from the group of native Dragon flyers surrounding him and grinned at Eegan. "The queen has returned and brought a king as well."

Arthur nodded seriously, leaving Joslin to reply.

"Well, you know, it has come to that point," Joslin told him.

"*Si, si,*" Pepe acknowledged with a twinkle in his eye.

"Is it winter in the Great Lakes region?" she asked.

"The Greats Lakes will be frozen over within two months," Pepe informed her.

"Good, we have some time to train and become better acquainted," she replied.

"I'll show you the spare rooms. You can take your pick and make yourself comfortable," he said, leading her down a hidden corridor at the opposite end of the room.

"The Dragon flyers from the abandoned sea cave will be joining us here," Joslin told Pepe.

"There are more spare rooms in the other pyramids," Pepe offered. "We'll find a place for everyone and every Sea Dragon. Tomorrow you can confer with Imaile."

Two months later the first group of Dragon flyers flew to the caves in the surrounding sandstone and limestone cliffs. Some of the caves led to deep underwater sea caves. The Drago flyers camped in the portion of the cave above water while many of the Sea Dragons quartered in the area underwater. They surfaced occasionally to meet with caretakers for hygiene and food. Scouts remained at the highest points to watch the Grays congregate on the snowy beaches. They were landing on the beaches in winged jets that reflected the moonlight bouncing off the clouds. They seemed unaware of the growing army of Sea Dragons beneath the frozen waters.

Joslin joined the scouts on the dawn of winter solstice. She, Arthur, and Eegan surveyed the region, and they finalized their plans. When the night came, Joslin observed Regulus rising in the clear, dark sky. The Grays had been attacking the Wise Kings, and their connection with the star station. Freeing Eegan had released them from entrapment as well, though they never would have realized it until much later. They would have been wandering the Gobi Desert forever, siphoning valuable energy from their star station until they were vulnerable to attack by the traitors, who would have easily devoured them shortly before destroying the star. When Regulus came close to Venus, Joslin gave the command for action. The starlight illuminated the beached Grays and made them easy targets. Several bands of Dragon flyers headed for the planes and sawed the wings off of them. They dismantled every piece of machinery in the area. Other Dragon flyers flew over the frozen lake and their Sea Dragons blew fire to melt the ice. More Sea Dragons poured from the depths of the lake through the melted openings. They attacked the Grays, who went scurrying for their equipment in panic.

Joslin met Arthur and Eegan at the giant gray crystal that drove the power station controls on the Gray's spacecrafts. The center of the crystal was embedded in a rocky crevice. There were gray petals folded around the center like the bud of a flower. The crystal resembled a flower that opened its petals in the morning and closed its petals at night. Unlike the Serpentines, the Grays preferred operating in daylight. Joslin had noticed this pattern over the years, and now she finally knew why. They were unable to obtain energy from the closed flower crystal at night. Elissa ejected a stream of fire from her mouth and melted the ice surrounding the grey petals. Joslin steadied her metal rod in the opening until the ice reformed, holding the rod securely upright. Then she and the others took cover behind some metal debris. Joslin grabbed a stick that had been lying on the ground and offered it to Elissa to light. The golden Sea Dragon queen gave a little puff, lighting the stick on fire.

Joslin now wielded a flaming torch. She threw it over the hollow opening of the metal rod. Then she ducked behind a pile of metal rubbish that had once been a winged jet. The flame from the torch ignited the gas inside the cavity of the metal rod. Within moments the metallic rod appeared translucent as the fire spiral down the tube into the crevice. The flame heated the gray crystal, which Joslin surmised had been filled with argon gas. The gray crystal suddenly emitted a soft blue-green light for a few minutes before dying into dark purple. Eegan, Joslin, and Elissa glanced at the dark night sky above them. Regulus had already completed its transit many degrees past Venus. Several pale purple supernovas appeared in the black sky. They flashed across the galaxy like a row of upright cards falling down in a series.

Joslin cleared the area to avoid asphyxiation and exposure in case there were unexpected explosions between the gas and metal. Both Sea Dragons and flyers paused briefly to view the spectacle in the night sky. The star Regulus seemed to twinkle a little brighter with an affirmative power surge, as if it had gathered energy from the effects of the supernovas rippling through space. Once those on the ground acknowledged the shift, the star resumed its original brightness.

"Let's go back to camp," Joslin said. "We can clean up this mess in the morning. There is only a residual left. Looks like we destroyed the Grays' terrestrial bases."

"The planetary stations remain, but a major one went up in smoke tonight," Elissa agreed as she sped through the clear darkness of the night back to the cliffs.

Chapter Twenty

If you have to sell out

For a song

The deal

Isn't worth it

Tune Reference: *A Whiter Shade Of Pale*

----Procol Harum

"IT WILL TAKE us at least another thousand years before we gather the momentum to destroy the stellar Serpentine base," Joslin commented as the Sea Dragons carried the remaining metal debris to the depths of the ocean. She and Arthur watched the scrap metal go down, down, down until only their reflections were visible on the ocean's surface. "We'll let the Light Beings inhabiting the deep decompose the rest."

Then she turned to the smoldering terrain left on the beach. The flora was devastated and giant scorch marks remained. Hazardous chemical goo oozed from the giant crystal and puddles were left where the winged jets had been destroyed. Joslin took her staff to one of the scorched areas. Placing it in the middle of the burnt grass, the metal rod glowed until a one hundred-square-foot area had been restored. Millions of tiny microbes rose to consume the toxins and till the ground. This process took approximately three days. Then earth spirits scattered grass seed. Wild beasts in the area brought other kinds of seeds from regional vegetation. The seeds clung to their fur coats for a free ride. Some of the beasts rolled in the newly tilled earth and the seeds released their grip.

After over a month's worth of work, a series of noiseless lightning flashed across the sky.

"It's the Thunder People," Joslin remarked to Arthur.

A sudden clap of rolling thunder added emphasis to her words. Arthur's eyes lit up like the brightest of stars. A sense of wonder shot across his countenance and brought peace.

"They want us to take a rest from the effects of the cleanup," Joslin translated. "It can have a secondary devastating effect."

More lightning streaked across the sky.

"There's more," Joslin observed.

The thunder pounded in the affirmative.

"There's a big storm coming. It is bringing in something. Something odd. We need to stay on alert," Joslin relayed.

"Witness the healing power of nature." Arthur brightened with a nod before speculating, "I wonder what the storm will fish in?"

A fierce ice storm came on the heels of the Thunder People. Joslin and the other Dragon flyers waited it out inside the caves on the cliff. The winds scattered the seeds of more vegetation and redistributed wildlife. Winter fowl, moles, chipmunks, and other small creatures washed up on the beach and were found by the Dragon flyers during ebbs in the storm. Some required minimal care while others simply scurried away to take refuge behind rocks or in holes in the ground. When the torrential rain and ice compelled them to go back inside the caves, Joslin and the others explored the cavities for openings and tunnels to other parts of the world.

"A Gray jet just landed on the beach," one of the scouts announced as he hurried into the cavern that Joslin was investigating. "It blew in with the last storm and almost crashed into the lake."

Joslin looked up from a map that had been drawn of the cave's passageways. "Didn't they get the message?"

"Apparently not, but they are no longer Gray. One is pink and the other one is aquamarine. There are only two. They seem to be trying to find the crystal flower."

"Let's go explain everything to these mutant Grays," Joslin told Eegan. "We'll send five of the other Dragon flyers to clip their wings."

Eegan hid under Joslin's camouflage cloak and they flew together on Elissa. The Sea Dragon found her way through the torrential rain and hail to the beach. The other Dragon flyers had already arrived to dismantle the jet. The Sea Dragons used their wings to slice the metal. The sound of power saws, the smell of melting metal, and the sight of the rising flames caught the attention of the two wandering Grays.

"Hey, Oscar, someone is clipping the wings off our jet!" the pink Gray shouted.

"Where is that gray flower?" Oscar lamented. He searched the restored terrain around the former site of the crystal. "I feel lost without it, as if somebody took out my heart."

"Forget the heart!" the pink Gray yelled. "Somebody just took our wings."

"I came to love that little gray jet," Oscar, who also had become accustomed to ignoring his crewmate, sighed. "Who would do something like that?"

"Hold it right there!" Joslin commanded, appearing before them from under her camouflage.

"Oh my gosh. It is a girl with a big rod!" the aquamarine Gray shouted.

Joslin swirled her metal rod, blocking their run for the snowy hills. Eegan joined her side as a wizened old man.

"She's got her old man with her!" the pink Gray exclaimed in terror. "He's probably a druid wizard."

"Drop your lasers," Joslin said as she pointed the hollow end of her metal rod at the chest of each Gray in an alternating rhythm.

The Grays became speechless. It suddenly dawned on them why they had been unable to connect with the heart of their operations.

"Come to Jesus!" Eegan began.

"Come to who?" Oscar, the aquamarine Gray, asked.

"We are here to put the fear of God in you," Eegan continued.

"Don't worry. We are scared already," confessed the pink Gray with a quiver.

"Good," Eegan said in a smooth, velvety voice. "Jesus saves."

"Can we be saved?" Oscar whimpered. He was almost on his knees.

"Apparently so. You are no longer gray," Eegan continued, stating the obvious.

"Thanks be to God!" the pink Gray exclaimed, closing his eyes and pleading with the universe.

"It's a miracle," Oscar said, seriously examining his new aquamarine color. "I see the light."

"Jet is de-winged," McGrail announced as he joined the group.

"Thanks be to God!" the pink Gray repeated.

McGrail studied the colored Grays. "Looks like we have a rainbow after the storm."

"They found the light," Joslin dryly replied. "It's a transformation."

McGrail scratched his head. "I see what we are up against."

"Take us with you!" the pink Gray cried. "I don't want to go back to that boring, drab color scheme. I can't handle the gray anymore. Color my world!"

"All we do is fight. I am tired of it," Oscar added.

"What is your name, Pink?" Eegan asked in a firm voice. He wanted to determine whether there was any brightness left in this Gray.

The pink Gray began sobbing hysterically. "Nobody ever asked me my name. I've always been just a number in the crowd. "He fell to his knees and cried.

"Our society is depersonalized," Oscar explained unemotionally. "We have numbers mostly, depending on the occasion."

"I was only calling Oscar by name to get on his nerves," the pink Gray wailed.

"Ask for forgiveness," Eegan insisted.

"His name is Gaul," Oscar mentioned. "He is one of many."

"Gaul, your new name is Paul," Eegan announced as Joslin and McGrail rolled their eyes. "Now ask your brother's forgiveness. Kiss and make up."

The heavy rain turned to snow. Oscar and Paul kissed and hugged each other. They began dancing under the falling white snowflakes.

"Let's get out of here," Joslin said, feeling annoyed at their ignorance.

"What do we do with these guys?" McGrail asked.

"Turn them into missionaries and send them back to the Grays' outposts," Joslin said softly. "They can say that they have been changed."

"Good idea," McGrail agreed. "What do we do with them until they become missionaries?"

Joslin turned her attention to the dancing Grays. She took a deep breath before she addressed them. "Hey, boys, we'll make a trade. We'll tell you about Jesus and you can tell us about your jet's cockpit."

Eegan grinned and winked at Joslin. "We could use the additional knowledge in reconstructing our Stonehenge grid system."

Joslin told McGrail, "Stay with the other Dragon flyers. Watch Paul and Oscar until they are ready to convert their brothers. Learn what you can about their technology. Meanwhile, get them to make a cozy shelter out of the remains of their jet. We can get rid of it later."

McGrail smiled at her plan and added more to the bargain. "I gather that Eegan will come and deliver weekly sermons at worship services?"

Paul and Oscar nodded eagerly. "It's a deal!"

Chapter Twenty-One

Chances, changes, and break aways
Take us to memories of loved ones

Tune Reference: *Breakaway*

----Kelly Clarkson

WHILE MCGRAIL AND his team educated Paul and Oscar, Joslin continued mapping the caverns connecting the sea caves.

"I think that the real miracle is finding the tunnel to MidEarth," Joslin remarked as she slapped her hands together to shake off the dirt.

"The connection already exists," Eegan replied. He had just returned from the beach. "Those transformed aliens have missed all this for years. They don't have a clue what spiritual treasures are here."

"It is all underneath the surface of their former reality," Joslin added. "Looks like we'll be moving Shambala. For the future, Shambala will be found in an area known as the Canadian Rockies. It will just be gridded differently so that the residual Grays left on Earth won't be able to find it."

"We have new Sea Dragons cocooning in the Great Lakes," Eegan announced.

"One of the Sea Dragons found an underwater tunnel from the Great Lakes to a freshwater lake in the Scottish Highlands," Joslin elaborated. "Signs of interconnectedness and new life are all around us. I think that our world is getting smaller."

"The Stonehenge network exists in the tunnels of the earth, not only in the energy of the mountain peaks," Eegan observed.

"I leave for Khotan tomorrow," Joslin informed him. "We think that there is another entrance to MidEarth nearby. I'll pay a visit to the baby Sea Dragons before I leave."

The next day Elissa took Joslin to the collection of Sea Dragon cocoons in a pristine section of the lake. It was early spring and some of the snow and ice had started to melt, leaving patches of tender green on the dark earth. They spotted a cocoon fragment on rocks near the cliffs. There was only one hatchling standing alone in the middle of the nest. It was a bright, flaming orange Sea Dragon.

"Oh, it's Nessie!" Elissa cried. "Where are the others?"

"Those traitors!" Nessie answered with a touch of indignation. "I barely escaped with my life from the Scottish Highlands."

Elissa and Joslin landed on the rocks at Nessie's side. They quickly scoured the area for other hatchlings but found only Nessie. Meanwhile, they began to fathom the recent betrayals, which caught them by surprise.

"Tell us what happened!" Elissa demanded of the newborn Sea Dragon as she sat down next to Nessie.

"I was getting ready to cocoon in Loch Oich with the rest of the pod when several Dragon flyers canoed toward us. They were wearing masks so that I could not see their faces. The rest swam to join them, but I remained motionless. Something seemed eerie about the intrusion and the diversion. One of the Dragon flyers opened his mouth to speak to the serpents, and I noticed that he had fangs. So I quickly swam toward Loch Ness, and all of them pursued me. When they realized that I was escaping, they drew their swords to kill me. Being smaller than the rest, I slipped behind some rocks at the bottom of Loch Ness. There, I found the tunnel that leads to the Great Lakes, and I cocooned in safety."

Elissa shuddered after hearing the story. "They have gone over to the Serpentines."

Joslin rose from the boulder where she had been perched. "There is no time to loose. I may not understand what is going on, but I know that we must continue with our mission to grid the planet with the new energy. The Serpentines are pressing on us because we destroyed the Grays' base. They lost an important ally." Then she addressed Nessie, "Do you know why the others went over?"

"They promised them immortality," Nessie answered.

"Don't they know that is a delusion?" Joslin asked. "Serpentines don't die; they can evaporate though, if the reflection is correct."

She paced a few steps along the edge of the rocks. She wondered what they had been thinking. Those who degenerated eventually passed into another dimension where they dissipated their energies into more than one transformation.

"I think that they got scared like the others who turned and allowed their insecurities to get the better of them," Elissa added. "These are not easy times."

"Oh," Joslin said, thinking over Elissa's words. She realized that she had been too preoccupied to notice the difficulty. Joslin gazed at the horizon and shuddered. "This is not the first power struggle associated with the Druid Isle. An investigation needs to be launched so that we know King Dadgon's loyalties."

Her thoughts were interrupted by the appearance in the sky of several Sea Dragons and flyers. She recognized Eegan riding with Merlin on his Sea Dragon. Pepe and the Latino Sea Dragons were accompanying them.

"The Serpentines are on to us," Eegan announced. "Time to scram. Some of the Dragon flyers suggest taking Paul and Oscar to the base in Mexico for further training. We've destroyed our traces. The Serpentines will wonder what happened, though they might suspect us. The Grays were always susceptible to self-destruction, being just a number to the Serpentine Federation."

"Are the gnomes, fairies, leprechauns, and merpeople securely established in the area?" Joslin inquired.

"*Si, senora*," Pepe replied. "As long as they minimize interactions with humans, the Serpentines will never find them."

Joslin brightened. "Are they able to freely travel to MidEarth when necessary?"

"No *problemo*," Pepe stated. "We left the tunnel unblocked."

"OK, let's go with plan B," Joslin encouraged. "Eegan's group sets up Shambala with a star seed colony called First Nations. They agreed to help hide the new site from the Serpentines. Start at the wide, stony, shallow crossing at the Red Deer River, and then look up for the best place. The First Nation people will meet you there."

Eegan appeared relieved that the groundwork for his new hideaway had already been established. "Can Oscar and Paul come with us until they are ready to slip across the Atlantic and preach to the Grays in Europe?"

"Sounds like a plan," Joslin, who desperately wanted to break away, rejoiced. Her ability to see into issues provided her with the remaining details that solidified her next plan. "We need Merlin to investigate the Lake Oich marauders. The rest of us will take the tunnel from the Great Lakes that goes through MidEarth into the portal by the Great Wall. From there, we'll cross the Gobi Desert and divert the Serpentines' attention from this area. Then we'll scramble over to Khotan before looking for new Sea Dragons in Lake Hovsgol."

"Finding Nessie here inspired us," Elissa added, nodding her golden head. Nessie looked up at the collection of Dragon flyers and Sea Dragons around her.

"Your caretaker will be a collective from MidEarth," Joslin explained, leaning down to speak to the small baby Sea Dragon. "The collective will consist of a gnome, leprechaun, fairy, and a merperson. There will be four total to attend to all of your needs as you protect the passageway from Scotland to the Great Lakes."

Chapter Twenty-Two

Even those broken in spirit
Can find love

Tune Reference: *She Will Be Loved*
----Maroon 5

FOR SEVEN MONTHS, Joslin and her group journeyed through MidEarth and found the portal to a segment of the Great Wall located near the present town of Bishkek. Elissa flew out of the opening and met a beautiful, young Chinese maiden dressed in white robes. A white parrot fluttered around her and occasionally rested on a branch in the willow tree above the maiden.

"Hello, Kuan Yin," Elissa greeted her. "I see that you heard our plea to grid compassion into the Stonehenge network."

Joslin remained on Elissa's back as the Sea Dragon spoke to the woman. She had fallen asleep from sheer exhaustion during the last leg of the journey while Kuan Yin guided the group in her meditation under the willow tree. She waited patiently for them to surface.

Kuan Yin smiled and lifted Joslin off the back of the golden Sea Dragon. "My teacher, Avalokiteshvara, from the Valley of Indus, told me that you needed me. I came to protect you from the Serpentines patrolling the desert." Then she bowed slightly, "I am returning the favor."

Joslin stirred and opened her eyes, blinking at the immortal time traveler in white robes.

"Joslin, this is Kuan Yin," Elissa said as introduction. "She is a time traveler. Brunswick, Earl, and myself protected her during her ascendance many years ago. She was one of the Arctos children that died as a result of the Serpentine experiments. She missed the airlift by the Santas by a year, otherwise she would have survived."

Joslin curiously approached the woman. "My father was named for the Arctos. His mother named him Arcas."

"Kuan Yin knows how to use the waveguide that the Santas created, and she maintains immunity from Serpentine intrusions. That's how she was able to guide us to the opening."

"We must hurry. The Serpentines sense your presence," Kuan Yin added. "We can disguise ourselves and follow the Silk Road to Khotan, where you will be safe under their meditative bubble."

"I'll go with Elissa while the others remain in MidEarth for safety," Joslin decided. "Once their passage is assured, then they can join us. I don't want to risk what has been accomplished so far."

Kuan Yin silently nodded and gently motioned Joslin down the Silk Road. The golden Sea Dragon queen walked beside them, occasionally scavenging for food along the way. They made most of their journey during dusk and twilight. This afforded them the most protection with the use of the camouflaging armor. Resting around the hours of noon and midnight, they managed to avoid detection as they crossed the Gobi Desert. They traded with several caravans and hid the golden Sea Dragon queen behind sand dunes while they exchanged the jewels from some of her scales for water and supplies. Elissa could always regrow the jewels on scales from the crystals they found in the sand. Many of the traders recognized the jewels as dragon tears, which was the term for gems that arose from their scales. The prized gems brought a good market price, and they never questioned the two women, who they knew were enlightened. They merely smiled and quietly traded with a sense of awe and wonder, which lent an air of peace and goodwill to the next people they encountered further down the road. This sense of abundance spread to the surrounding oasis communities, and people quit fighting amongst themselves. There was magic in the air, and though nobody ever talked about the two women walking alone on the Silk Road, the appearance of the dragon tears in day-to-day barter spoke to the hearts of everyone involved in the commerce of the Silk Road. Many had already heard of Kuan Yin, which literally translated into Sacred Temple of the Feminine.

People in the caravans were amazed to see her traveling with a redheaded stranger with clear blue eyes that could see miles away in the thickest of desert storms. Kuan Yin spoke for the stranger in the languages of the local inhabitants, and this opened their hearts to Joslin. Joslin was moved deeply by their hospitality, which responded to the elegant grace of Kuan Yin. They knew the story of her ascendance from the Serpentine capture and how she returned in another lifetime as the beautiful wife of Siddhartha Guatama. The alchemical cultivation of her spirit during the Serpentine capture had brought her to a rare state of enlightenment that overwhelmed the prince, who lived in a perfect world. He was not on the same level, and left her to achieve his own state of enlightenment. The world already knew her as the compassionate time traveler who sent the white dove with an olive branch to Noah after the floodwaters had begun to recede. The olive branch carried rice seeds. The dove dropped the rice seeds on the fur of

Noah's dog, which scattered the seeds in the muddy water. She became known in a later lifetime as Yasodhara. Her spiritual teacher, Avalokiteshvara, encouraged her to learn about love after her experiences with the Serpentines. It was the next step in spiritual wholeness. Although she had been groomed to marry her cousin, Prince Siddhartha, she and the betrothed prince fell in love. As a result, she could not hide her spiritual strength, and he felt intimidated by it. Instead of raising himself up to her level, he rejected her and pursued his own religion. Yasodhara took the high road as she had done during her former lifetime as one of the Arctos. She converted to her husband's new religion and became a nun, bringing her innate spirituality down to earth rather than ascending.

By the time the two women and Sea Dragon reached Khotan, Joslin had learned many words in the native languages and how to safely travel the Silk Road. The mediating population of Khotan was impressed, as usual, by their arrival. This time they relished sharing much of their day-to-day life with Joslin. No longer was she just a high-flying traveler on a golden creature, but she appeared more engaging and participated in village life. She helped prepare food, wash clothes, watch youngsters, and tend crops. Joslin wanted to know everything about their lives and how they thrived in the desert. For Joslin, these endeavors served as relief from her heady thoughts on world affairs and their present predicament. Sometimes she found that solutions and revelations arose out of the most mundane activities.

After a week Elissa pushed the women to leave the comfort of Khotan and press on. "There are new cocoons in Lake Hovsgol," she urged them. "You've taught the villagers how to maintain the security of the Silk Road in their meditations, and it's time to press further. We need to establish a new base and I know just the people who can protect it."

Joslin and Kuan Yin looked at the golden Sea Dragon queen curiously. Elissa was not going to elaborate until they had reached their destination. They remembered those who had been left behind in MidEarth for protection. Now that Elissa had hinted at a solution, they felt more inclined to proceed with their plans. They left early the next morning, hours before the break of dawn.

Four months later they crossed over the last mountain and reached Lake Hovsgol, a crystal-blue lake.

"I'll leave you to your search for the cocooning Sea Dragons," Kuan Yin announced. "You are safe here, and I have work to do elsewhere."

Joslin embraced the time traveler and said good-bye before she disappeared over the mountains. Then she and Elissa flew over the lake, looking for possible cocoons. At the mouth of a clear mountain stream, they spotted several small baby Sea Dragons waving at them.

"There they are!" Joslin shouted excitedly to Elissa. The sighting of the fresh, young Sea Dragons was the best news of the past two years. Then, out of the corner of her eye, she spotted a tall, hairy, erect beast ducking for cover under some fir trees. "What was that!" she exclaimed.

Elissa abruptly landed next to the baby Sea Dragons before responding. "THAT is our best protection."

Joslin stared at the area where the hairy beast had disappeared. She remained motionless for several seconds, and then she turned her attention to the new Sea Dragons. They were unlike any others that she had seen. These new Sea Dragons were shorthaired and without scales. They had the face of a magnificent dragon but the body of a lion, complete with pointed tail. Their wings were smaller than the others, and Joslin realized that they would grow to only six or seven feet tall, rather than the typical twelve to fourteen feet of the average Sea Dragon. Not only did they resemble a feline, but these Sea Dragons also purred. Several of the hatchlings wrestled with each other on the soft needles covering the forest floor. These Sea Dragons lacked the vibrant colors of their predecessors: they all had light tan fur.

"These little ones like to play," Joslin observed as two baby Sea Dragons tumbled over Elissa's feet.

"Yes, I know," Elissa sighed, tossing the babies lightly in the air with a soft kick. "They were always that way, even as serpents in Atlantis."

Joslin counted seven new Sea Dragons. They somersaulted in the air and danced around her. Four of them erupted into a Hopak, demonstrating a dance that the descendants of the native Dragon flyers would learn as the Cossack dance.

"Quit complaining," a Sea Dragon said as he nudged Elissa's shoulder with a high jump. "It keeps us in shape and warm in winter. You gotta be light on your feet to live so close to the Serpentines' base and experimental lab."

Elissa laughed at the prancing Sea Dragon. "You are right, Jacob. You all are very well-suited for the job that lies ahead of us."

Joslin overheard their conversation and glanced at Elissa for an explanation. The golden Sea Dragon queen was not forthcoming with information. Instead she laughed and joined the dancers around her, clapping her hands together for a beat. Realizing that it was hopeless to pursue any further conversation, Joslin contented herself with constructing a small fire to keep warm and elicited flames from the baby Sea Dragons. When the wood caught fire, she perched on a rock and watched the dancing while munching on some small cakes from her latest trade on the Silk Road.

Several hours after sundown, the new caretakers for the baby Sea Dragons arrived. They had slightly pronounced foreheads with hairy limbs and torsos, and they closely resembled the tall, erect creature she had spotted darting under the forest canopy. She noticed that all the new caretakers were male.

"They are refugees from the villages that the Serpentines attacked. They raped the women, killed the men, and exiled the younger males. They stigmatized the exiled males as untouchables after they tattooed a permanent six-pointed star on them."

Joslin intently studied the emerging group of young men around her. She finally made out a six-pointed star under the nape of the neck of a young man standing quietly next to her. He struck her as handsome with very benign, refined features. She could not imagine any human being referring to this viral group of eligible bachelors as untouchable. She blushed slightly as the young man next to her acknowledged her attention. He beamed at her.

"How long have they been exiled?" Joslin asked Elissa.

"They have been wandering the mountains for over four years. They have already created their own military group, though they come to us as caretakers to heal the wound of the exile."

Joslin's sharp eyes noticed a tall, hairy figure dashing around in the forested shadows of the campfire. "Looks like our protection is around."

Elissa smiled at the group of young men, "Your parents are always nearby." Then she remarked to Joslin, "The Serpentines attacked only half of the parents. The others are Neanderthal, and they remain on the outskirts of the forests, continually eluding the Serpentines as they have for thousands of years. Like the Lemurians, this particular star seed civilization refused to participate in the human experiments with the Serpentines. Over the years they have created their own mutations to blend in on their own terms. They still refuse to wear clothes and allow their hair to grow like an animal's fur to stay warm."

"They have pronounced frontals," Joslin added, probing Elissa for more explanations.

"They have a highly sophisticated limbic system, which is intricately connected to their cortex," Elissa continued. "With our input, they created their own equivalent to the reptilian brain. In a compassionate gesture, they seeded it into the human brain. It is a portion of the brain that has not been activated, though."

"How did they manage to do that?" Joslin questioned as she glanced silently at the men who had left her side to collect the young Sea Dragons. In comparison to the other caretakers, these were very attentive and gentle.

"Their version is a reflection of the impulse that created the planet," Elissa answered. "It is present in every earth and water spirit. They grew this portion of the brain from the same holographic mirror network that served as the basis for the Santas' waveguide."

Joslin pondered this information as she bedded down for the night. The caretakers took shifts caring for the new Sea Dragons throughout the night. The next day she awoke and explored the area with Elissa. They found a network of caves with tunnels to the Altai Mountains. Joslin and the caretakers wasted no time in moving the Sea Dragons to this honeycombed network. In one of the tunnels, they found several dead bodies that had been preserved for over ten thousand years by the cold.

"We found the Arctos," Elissa observed. "I bet there are more bodies in these caverns."

"They seem unharmed except for the blood coming from their ears," Joslin observed. "The Serpentines hit them with a high-intensity laser. However, these mountains didn't collapse like some of the others."

"Maybe they were on the fringe of the laser's range," Elissaxs speculated. She began devouring one of the frozen corpses.

"Looks like the cleanup crew has already started," Joslin commented. She was more than happy to have the area cleared immediately. The Sea Dragons were scavengers as well as protectors. She didn't savor the idea of running into more grim reminders of the past. "We'll send the baby Sea Dragons to this tunnel. Let me know if you find anything interesting before you eat it for lunch."

Then she hurried back down the path she came, leaving Elissa alone to forage through the labyrinth of caves that had once belonged to the Arctos. She arrived at the entrance near Lake Hovsgol and scouted for the new Sea Dragons. Much to her surprise, she found a familiar face instead.

"Hello there, Joslin," Kuan Yin greeted her. "I heard that you've discovered the former home of the Arctos. It was once my home in another lifetime."

"Apparently, you are still connected," Joslin observed. "How did you know?"

"Elissa summoned me," the time traveler answered. "We maintain our connection through the old Santas' waveguide."

"Oh, that's right," Joslin replied, still in shock from her findings farther up the cave. "I think you told me that."

She brewed herself a cup of tea from her collection of local herbs and offered a cup to Kuan Yin. Then she sat down on a stone inside the cave and reflected on her findings. Kuan Yin sipped her cup of tea after sitting down on a rock beside her.

"How long have you been investigating these caverns?" Kuan Yin asked.

"About five months now," Joslin answered before changing the subject. "How far away is the Serpentine Federation laboratory?"

"It is just over the mountains," Kuan Yin replied.

"Time to pay the Serpentines a visit," one of the caretakers interrupted as he entered the cave.

Joslin recognized Yuri, the young man who had stood beside her on that first day that the new Sea Dragons' caretakers had arrived. The Sea Dragons were almost mature now, though they had not finished settling into the new cave yet.

"Are the new Sea Dragons ready, Yuri?" Joslin asked.

"Yes, I think so," Yuri answered. "It is time to get on with it."

"It does seem that we have come full circle today," Joslin noted, and she glanced at Kuan Yin for her agreement.

"The Serpentines returned to the laboratory after the Castle Marlboro fell," Kuan Yin mentioned. "Although the world had already learned of their experiments, they persisted in their efforts to seed themselves into humanity."

"Except this time, they have been successful," Yuri observed.

"Will the caretakers accompany me in attacking the Serpentine lab?" Joslin asked.

"That's why the new Dragon flyers have not arrived yet," Yuri smiled. "We are prepared to battle those responsible for our exile. It is part of our community dharma."

Kuan Yin nodded. "Elissa asked me here to help with the cleanup of the laboratory. It is a healing process for me, and I can serve as a guide."

Joslin gulped her tea. "Elissa is an optimist. Stay here, Kuan Yin, until we have flushed the Serpentines out of the lab. Yuri, tell the others that we leave in two weeks. Meanwhile, I am going to have a word or two with Elissa."

Yuri smiled and nodded, and then he hurriedly left to tell the others.

"Did someone call my name?" Elissa questioned as she emerged from the dark confines of the cave.

"How do you figure that we stand a chance against the Serpentines?" Joslin pointedly asked the golden Sea Dragon queen.

Kuan Yin smiled. "I'll answer that for you, Elissa." Then she turned towards Joslin and addressed her. "You have a different sort of protection this time."

"What is it?" Joslin quizzed.

"Love," Kuan Yin responded. "Yuri is in love with you."

Elissa nodded at Joslin, and she blushed slightly. She recalled her attraction to him and how much she enjoyed sitting around the campfire with him long after the others had gone to bed. She had not realized her feelings until this moment.

"And I have fallen in love with him," Joslin admitted. "Let's hope that is enough."

Chapter Twenty-Three

Balance the goals

With the process of attainment

Tune Reference: *It's The Climb*

----Miley Cyrus

JOSLIN TIGHTLY PRESSED Yuri's hand in hers before she climbed on Elissa's back. Though she never mentioned her feelings to him, she focused on their interactions. She wasn't ready to complicate her life any more than the present circumstances permitted, preferring to allow the relationship to take its natural course. He felt her touch and lightly kissed her forehead in return. Assured that she was special in his life, Joslin steadied herself on the golden Sea Dragon queen and softly blew him a kiss. He smiled his receipt. Flying high above the snow-covered mountains, Joslin sincerely hoped that she lived to see another day and be with him again. The rest of the group followed behind her in "V" formation like a band of migrating birds. She saw Yuri smiling to himself in his position at one of the ends. They encircled the Serpentine lab at the base of the mountains and dismounted.

The Sea Dragons blew flames at the snow base, causing a layer of steam to rise from the rapidly melting snow. It enveloped the Serpentines' building until it was covered in a dense fog, making visibility no greater than a few feet. Tiny streams emerged from the higher ground and ran collectively toward the building. Soon the Serpentine building was underneath two feet of rising water. Almost-human Serpentines ran out of the building, gasping for air, as the Sea Dragons puffed in their direction; the caretakers and Joslin remained above the smoke and flooding waters. Joslin watched the commotion below with the acute vision that the Sea Dragons had imparted to her during training exercises. The lithe, new Sea Dragons quickly pounced on any Serpentine that escaped the circle of fog and smoke.

When Joslin allowed the smoke to clear, they rushed the building from all directions and poured into all entrances. Joslin detected no signs of life as she hurriedly toured the laboratory. The bodies of almost-human Serpentines lay strewn across the floors in every room. She was surprised by the numbers and how closely their features resembled the human form. She could tell by the expressions on their faces that they had not gone beyond their instincts in responding to the attack. They never knew what hit them, whether it had been their own undoing or an intruder.

"I think that we have accomplished our mission," Joslin told Elissa. "Tell the Yeti to cover the area with their protective grid before the other Serpentines come looking for their laboratory. Then we'll put it in another dimension for safekeeping as we transmute it. Some of the Yeti may need rides to the Great Lakes, Red Deer, and Pacific Northwest to help tie in the protective grid."

Elissa smiled thoughtfully. "It is a great day for the Yeti. I can remember when their Neanderthal ancestors first landed here after the Serpentines destroyed their planet. They developed immunity from the Serpentines the hard way and don't mind sharing their talents with us."

Joslin grinned when she heard Elissa's words. The handsome caretakers were included in the list of Neanderthal descendants. She had grown fond of all of them, and she could not imagine a world without them.

"Oh," she added, "you and the Sea Dragons can just help yourself to Serpentine bodies. There is nothing worth keeping there, and I sure would hate to see them fall into the wrong hands for future cloning. It is one experiment worth eating. Just leave the lab equipment intact until Kuan Yin and I can finish our investigation. We'll just help ourselves to the technology while you feast."

Then she went outside the building and the caretakers followed her. Everyone knew that scavenging Sea Dragons did not always have the best table manners. Not only would the Sea Dragons eventually remove the bodies, but they would also clear the energy. This would allow them to conduct their investigation without shock or grimness. It would be transformed into an energetically inert area that could be transmuted into a new base for the Sea Dragons and other inhabitants.

Yuri caught Joslin off guard with a long, deep, passionate kiss after they had returned to their station on higher ground. Their backs were turned to the building below them, and they faced the white mountains. She relaxed in his embrace and returned his kiss.

The other caretakers left and began searching for shelter. They needed to find a place to board the Sea Dragons for the night after they finished eating. Ignoring the couple kissing on the side of the mountain, the caretakers found a cave that they suspected had once belonged to the Arctos. Nobody ventured very far into the cave, instead opting to go no farther than an empty cavern near the entrance. Further investigations could wait. Already it had been an emotionally trying day.

"I love you," Yuri whispered to Joslin when he stopped and gazed into her eyes.

Joslin closed her eyes and placed her cheek against his left ear before replying, "I love you."

Then she turned toward the valley below them, and wrapped her arm around his side.

Though heartbroken, Yuri deftly responded to her subtle brush-off by leaving the ledge to join the other caretakers. "It is time to call in the Sea Dragons for the night."

Joslin slowly turned around and noticed that Yuri was already halfway down the mountainside. She remained on the ledge and watched the sunset rays color the white mountains in shades of gold. Although the day appeared as golden as the scales on Elissa, she could not escape the feeling that something was missing. Something dear had been loss. The price paid for a single golden moment had been too high. A tear escaped her eye as she watched Yuri gather the eight Sea Dragons and directed them up the mountain.

She shook her head and resumed looking into the distant sunset until darkness fell. She wondered what Arthur, Wayne, and Eegan were doing now. She missed those familiar faces, especially the warm hearth in Wayne and Minerva's cottage. Two of the other caretakers came toward her moments later. She had been lost in memories of her former home and had not noticed their approach. Her present circumstances seemed stark and isolated in comparison.

"There is a brilliant fire warming the cavern now," Peter, one of the caretakers, announced.

Joslin appeared slightly startled by their intrusion into her thoughts, but she shrugged it off. She looked in the direction of the cavern for confirmation. Noticing a welcoming fire spewing smoke and flames out of the opening, she followed the caretakers silently across the mountain.

After several days of recuperation, Joslin and Elissa explored the mountains for a larger shelter. The cavern proved much smaller and shallower than anticipated. Within three weeks they had found a much larger cave with a dense shield of vines and moss covering the entrance. Though hidden from view behind several rock formations, the greenery was in sharp contrast to the snowy terrain. The bones of many different kinds of creatures were scattered across the floor in the entry. They wandered through the long hall that extended from the opening to a series of large rooms containing food, herbs, blankets, and other amenities. At the center of the array of rooms was a smaller room with a table and comfortable chairs. A large, round, blue gem, four feet in diameter, was mounted in a wooden frame near the far end of the table.

"It served as a communication device for the Arctos," Elissa mentioned as Joslin studied the polished blue rock. "Put your hand on the stone and summon Kuan Yin. She was an Arctos once. Let's see if she can remember how to tap into their communications network."

Joslin tried out Elissa's suggestion. She agreed that it was time to ask Kuan Yin to come and help reclaim the region from the Serpentines' grip. She also appreciated having another female to balance the group's energy, which was heavily masculine and slightly intimidating, though everyone had been very kind. She sighed, recalling the joyful sense of balance she had experienced at Camelon and in her younger years. She could not help but feel off in this environment with so many gloomy reminders of the past to sort and heal.

When she touched the stone and thought of Kuan Yin, a blue light emanated from the stone and filled the room. The image of Kuan Yin appeared from inside the stone, and Joslin saw her nod silently, accepting the essence of her message. The image and light faded a few seconds after Joslin dropped her hand from the stone's surface. Joslin stared into space for a few moments, pondering the sense of connection that she had just experience with Kuan Yin. A soft pain tugged at her heart as a distant memory rose to the surface. It had been a long time since she felt that connected to any creature, even Elissa. It was almost as if she had been going through the motions of life, never calling anyone for help or forming the type of attachment that extended across the ages. She slowly rose from her position beside the round, blue stone. As much as she had learned to see, Joslin felt blind.

"Let's go," Joslin told Elissa. Then she walked out of the room, feeling very much alone. She could tell that the former inhabitants had lived here very comfortably with happy families and tight communities. Touring the rooms, Joslin gathered as much information as she could about their lives. Elissa assumed a position several steps in front of Joslin and led her through many passageways that converged to a single point. At the heart of the living spaces was a large cavity that opened directly to the sky. A beautiful, warm pool stood under the opening. Wisps of steam rose from the hot springs and exited through the hole in the mountain.

"Oh, it's wonderful!" Joslin exclaimed, awestruck by the serenity of the landing pad, which had been the final resting place for many of the Arctos. She knew that they had died while waiting to be airlifted away from the deadly Serpentine lasers. There were no bodies left to tell the story, which had been transmitted through time by surviving storytellers. Instead, there was only beauty and hope left behind as their legacy.

Joslin sat down on the edge of hot springs and put her feet in the soothing water. Elissa jumped in the pool for a swim, diving underwater. Her golden scales shimmered in the pool's reflection, casting beams of light around Joslin. Suddenly Joslin no longer felt so alone. The spirit of the place called to her. She looked at the steam rising from the crystal-blue water. In the swirling vapor reaching for the sky, Joslin imagined a huge, thriving city filling the insides of the mountain.

Chapter Twenty-Four

Enjoy the loved ones

Who put on the day

By making every morning joyful

Tune Reference: *Chelsea Morning*

----Joni Mitchell

WHEN JOSLIN RETURNED to the cavern several days later, Kuan Yin greeted her.

"You called for my help," she told Joslin. "You must have used an ancient communications network."

Joslin excitedly nodded. "Yes, I need your guidance in the laboratory building. I want to figure out what to keep and what to destroy." Then she curiously looked at the goddess. "I think that we found the former headquarters for the Arctos."

Kuan Yin shook her head softly and looked down at the floor of the temporary shelter for the Sea Dragons. "I don't know," she replied earnestly. Then she raised her head and suggested, "Let's check out the laboratory tomorrow after we both have had a night's rest."

Joslin agreed and retired early that evening in an isolated space tucked far back in the cavern. She wanted to be alone with her thoughts. The encounter with Yuri had left her feeling awkward, straining her relationship with the others as well. She had crossed that subtle line into intimacy and nothing seemed the same anymore. She could not go back and change the past, nor could she find a way to move forward without a knot in her stomach for the present. Was it love that had earned her victory over the Serpentines?

The next day Joslin toured the Serpentine facilities with Kuan Yin. Entering the building for the first time since the raid, she noticed that the Sea Dragons had done a great job cleaning up the place. Now they could examine the artifacts and technology more objectively. She watched Kuan Yin sigh with relief that her memories associated with the site were not as painful as anticipated.

"When they began tormenting us after school ended, they locked us in these rooms according to gender and maturation. Some of my cellmates were impregnated, but none of the embryos survived. Some women died during the miscarriages from loss of blood. Despite all of their technical sophistication, the Serpentines did not know how to keep a human body healthy. Some of the girls went insane, which messed up their experiments because the Serpentines did not know the difference between sane behavior and the bizarre."

Joslin strolled through the cells and rooms alongside Kuan Yin. When they passed a particular room, she heard her companion gasp.

"I died in this cell," she said, slightly amazed from witnessing the overlay of lives. "It was terrible." Then Kuan Yin noticed the orange gemstone that Elissa had left for her in the corner of the room. She went over and picked it up. Rubbing the crystal between her fingers, she looked up at the window overhead. "The three Sea Dragons broke the window and accompanied my ascendance. The Serpentines had fled after I died. They were still in a frenzy and continued searching out others. I had pressed one of the control buttons so that they could not get to anyone else."

Joslin sat down on the floor of the room and sobbed. Her parents had also been tortured beyond relief on the earth plane. The Serpentines had been ultimately responsible for their demise. Now that she was older, she understood more of the implications. Kuan Yin sat down beside Joslin and stared into space.

Elissa suddenly appeared at the entrance to the room and helped Joslin to her feet. Yuri and several other caretakers stood beside the golden Sea Dragon queen. They escorted the young woman out of the cell.

"Come, Kuan Yin," Elissa said. "This time you walk out of this room alive and free. There are no threats anymore."

Kuan Yin rose to her feet. Lifting her head, she looked around with a smile.

"You are right," she answered calmly as she joined Elissa's side. "Let's go. I've had enough."

They went outside the building and were met by Peter, one of the caretakers who had accompanied Joslin. "Joslin asked me to tell you that she found nothing worth keeping. We raze the place tomorrow. Then we'll take care of the environmental impact."

Kuan Yin glanced at the golden Sea Dragon queen beside her. The dragon's scales glistened in the setting sun and cast a warm hue around them. The sight was spectacular against the backdrop of the snow-covered mountains. "That's a great idea. Restoring the site to its natural order would do a world of good."

Elissa and the caretaker smiled their agreement. Together they walked up the path to the mountain, where they met the others in the cavern. Joslin sat near Yuri by the campfire. He was strumming his oud, a mandolin-like instrument, and his melodious voice softly filled the cavern with a love song that he had composed for Joslin during the recent hiatus in their courtship. It was obvious from the expression on Joslin's face that he had completely won her over. Only the other caretakers knew that he played the oud and could sing.

Ivan, the Sea Dragon under Yuri's care, commented to Elissa and Kuan Yin when they entered the cavern, "Do you think I could get Yuri to sing me to sleep when he finishes entertaining Queen Joslin?"

Kuan Yin laughed at Ivan's jest. She added, "I don't think he's ready to quit anytime soon. You might have to wait until dawn to get your lullaby."

"Ah, it's tough being a Sea Dragon," Ivan moaned with a mock sigh.

Elissa jabbed him in the ribs. "Go to sleep. We get to raze the place tomorrow."

"Yee-hah!" Ivan murmured with delight. He did not want to disrupt Yuri, who had obviously healed his broken heart. Ivan had spent the past month coaching Yuri on how to deal with Joslin. He told Yuri that not only was Joslin a direct descendant of ol' King Cole, but that her parents and grandparents had been talented musicians.

"Music brought King Arthur's parents together," Ivan told Yuri. "It runs in the family."

Yuri took heed and composed his love song for Joslin. Then he waited for the perfect opportunity. Tonight belonged to Yuri.

Silence descended as Joslin kissed Yuri's lips. The others in the cavern hurried to their quarters to avoid disturbing her world, which for the moment appeared to center on Yuri. The young man put his oud aside and led her to a secluded area in the cavern. She stayed with him that night. They slept while the Sea Dragons razed the building early the next morning. Afterward, Joslin rose to begin the task of reclaiming the environment with her hollow staff while Yuri attended to Ivan when the Sea Dragon returned late that afternoon.

"How did it go last night?" Ivan, asked, noticing that Yuri seemed unusually quiet.

"Everything is fine," he answered without offering any additional information. He continued to groom the Sea Dragon in a happy, contented silence. Ivan felt that this was an improvement over Yuri's former mood and didn't press him further.

Later in the evening Joslin and Yuri moved into a smaller antechamber inside the new cave with the hot springs and landing pad.

"Those whom we sheltered in MidEarth will be arriving soon," Joslin said as they toured the cave. They searched for a space where they could live together and have relative privacy. "They will start new construction once they settle. The large cave is big enough for all our plans."

"Let's take one of the suites off the antechamber," Yuri suggested. "They are all plumbed with running hot water from the springs."

Joslin smiled and kissed his cheek. While she imagined the big picture, Yuri helped her find balance in the grander scheme. She looked forward to creating a new home with him. He softly grinned and centered himself at her receptivity to his offer.

"Let's bring our things for the night and settle in. The others will follow when they are ready, especially when they find out that this place is well-equipped and supplied," Yuri said. Then he added with a wry grin, "I know Ivan will come along just to check on us."

"That makes two Sea Dragons," Joslin counted. "Elissa will follow us tonight. She saw this coming before I did. Kuan Yin left to retrieve those from MidEarth. They will be under the protection of the Silk Road."

"Great, I can repair my hunting spear tomorrow morning with two fire-breathing Sea Dragons," Yuri continued. "I noticed a welding pit in the main cave. Iron tools are the latest craze. We could go into production and sell our products on the Silk Road."

Chapter Twenty-Five

Tiger eyes

Guard us all

Tune Reference: *Eye Of The Tiger*

----Survivor

"A LTTLE MORE on the right," Ivan said as Yuri groomed the fur on the tigerlike Sea Dragon.

He combed the soft fur around Ivan's neck. Suddenly the Sea Dragon turned and nuzzled his hand. Yuri stopped and glanced at the gift the Sea Dragon bestowed on him. Ivan had placed a gemstone into his palm. Yuri studied the stone carefully and held it against Ivan's face.

"It's a tiger's eye," Yuri exclaimed at the comparison.

"Wear it as an amulet around your neck for one hundred days," Ivan instructed before leaping to the top of a nearby rocky ledge to peer down at his caretaker.

Yuri stared into Ivan's deep, brown eyes and probed their depths. He found a tenacious spirit in their misty presence that captured him while freeing him at the same time. Yuri looked down and shook his head. He could not escape the impression that the Sea Dragon had given him. It seared the depths of his soul, imprinting a sense of indomitable fortitude. Yuri lifted his head and blinked at the Sea Dragon, who was sporting a mischievous grin.

Satisfied that his gift had been well-received, Ivan hopped down from the ledge and left Yuri alone in the cave.

Yuri walked outside into the light. His eyes swept the domain of the snowy mountains like an alert cat's. He could see beyond the protective bubble of the region and sensed the danger on the other side. For the first time, it didn't scare him. He could look at it squarely in the eye without flinching. He wondered at this new sense of self-assuredness. It felt like a new game, and he smiled when he recalled Ivan's mischievous grin. He now understood the importance of play.

He ran back into the cave and immediately searched for Joslin. His sight granted him the ability to find whatever he desired as if he possessed a bat-like sonar or all-knowingness. Joslin noticed the mirth in his face and concluded her conservation with the gnomes, who were constructing an office near the landing pad. He smoothly put his arm around her waist and drew her to him.

"You must come with me," he told her. Yuri ushered her outside of the cave after she left the gnomes with some final instructions.

Curious about Yuri's mood, Joslin followed him over the rocky terrain to an outpost behind some boulders. The excitement in his eyes bewildered and entranced her. She followed his line of sight and saw several familiar Dragon flyers making their way over the horizon.

"Yuri, how did you know?" she giggled in delight.

Her childhood friend Eegan and his life partner Pepe headed their way. Pepe's Sea Dragon, Taco, almost reached the safe confines of the protective bubble.

Yuri silently pointed to a dark speck in the sky. Several Dragon flyers working for the Serpentines had also seen them coming. They trailed Eegan and Pepe by 200 meters.

Joslin's face grew serious. She whistled softly for Elissa and the golden Sea Dragon appeared moments later. Pointing to the pursuit going on in the sky, Joslin told her, "They need cover. Summon the others."

Ivan suddenly appeared out of nowhere, and Yuri quickly mounted him, racing for the clouds overhead. Joslin waited for the others while Ivan hid in the clouds. When the assailants passed underneath, the Sea Dragon pounced on them and tore out the throats of the reptilian dragons with his mighty claws. Yuri swiftly toppled the traitorous flyers and they fell to the earth. Then they hid in the clouds again until they were sure that there were no others. The other Sea Dragons remained at the edge of the protective bubble until Ivan and Yuri met them. Later they joined Eegan and Pepe at the landing pad, and they thanked them for providing safety.

"We can always outrun them," said Pepe, who knew that he had been named appropriately. "Especially speedy Gonzalez. It's always better, though, if you kill them. One less out there waiting to kill you."

Eegan eyed his life partner silently. Pepe's words abruptly educated him on the reality of the situation. The Dragon flyers from the base at Teotihuacán experienced a rougher side of life than he cared to admit.

"I really miss my Tibetan mountaintop with the Golden Flowers," Eegan admitted.

"That's is exactly why we need you here," Joslin said as she appeared on the landing pad with Elissa.

She had overheard the last words of their conversation. Joslin greeted Eegan with a heart-filled hug. His appearance regained its youthfulness in her presence. At twenty-four years of age, he was four years older than Joslin.

"Send out the hungry Sea Dragons for cleanup," Joslin told the other Dragon flyers. "Provide cover from inside the protective bubble until all remaining evidence has been devoured."

"One of the bodies carried this," Yuri announced as he held a leather satchel up in front of Joslin.

Both Joslin and Eegan gasped.

"That belonged to my mother. She used it to carry medical supplies," Joslin said. She seized the satchel from Yuri's hand and hurriedly left the landing pad for her private quarters in the adjoining atrium. Before she left she planted a soft but voluptuous kiss on Yuri's lips.

"You made points with that find," Eegan commented as he patted Yuri on the back. "Good man."

"These catlike qualities pay off," Yuri said and winked at Ivan with a grin.

"*Si, senor*," Pepe added. "You shredded those traitors in the air."

"Time to sharpen our claws," Ivan replied. "Yuri, bring those swords that we have been working on. Meet you at the forge, unless Joslin attacks you while you look for the swords in the atrium."

Yuri spoke to Eegan as he shrugged at Ivan, "Do you ever feel that the Sea Dragons are trying to breed us instead of the other way around?"

Pepe burst into a hearty laugh before Eegan responded, "That is why I don't give them a chance."

Yuri grinned wryly as he pondered the alternative. "Well, she is beautiful."

"Don't do anything I wouldn't do," Eegan continued. "Swords can always wait. So can you. Free choice, free will."

"I think I am going outside to smell the flowers," Yuri decided as he wandered outside the cave.

"He's a fast learner," Ivan observed, cleaning his own claws.

"He knows his own mind," Pepe commented.

"Comes with the territory," Ivan added.

"I see that you have been mentally jousting with your caretaker-flyer," Pepe confronted.

"*Si, senor*," Ivan mimicked as he busily corrected a hangnail. "It will help Yuri hold his own with the powerful senora, not to mention those adversaries with the hypnotic slithery tongues and reptilian brains."

"It's called balance," Kuan Yin interrupted as she appeared from a portal in the mists. Like Joslin earlier, she had overheard the last words of the conversation.

"It's evolution," rephrased Merlin, suddenly appearing beside Kuan Yin in the portal and rubbing his head. "The Sea Dragons played a role in the development of the mammalian brain as well as my own rebirth."

"It's called hope," Arthur said. The king stepped out of the portal behind Merlin. "It tips the balance in our favor."

"He's a Westerner," Eegan explained as he gave the woman an affectionate a hug. "Instead of balance, they are into transcendence and attributes."

Kuan Yin smiled contentedly at his explanation. "There is more for me to learn."

"Hey, wait a minute," Pepe interjected, almost angrily. "How are you so familiar with this *senorita*?"

Eegan and Kuan Yin laughed. They stepped aside as Elissa stepped toward him to explain. Her soft manner calmed Pepe.

"Many past lives ago, Eegan and Kuan Yin enjoyed being brother and sister in Atlantis. After the Serpentines captured his younger sister, Eegan, known then as Landon, led a group to the high mountains of Tibet shortly before the Great Cataclysm sunk Atlantis. After his sister ascended, the relationship between brother and sister became timeless."

"You're *familia!*" Pepe exclaimed as he exuberantly embraced Kuan Yin. Then he stepped back and shouted to everyone standing around, "*Familia!*"

"Which reminds me," Arthur said abruptly. "Where is my sister?"

"Where is Joslin, my human sponsor?" Merlin asked dryly.

"Well, if you wait a moment, we might get what we all have been hoping for," Ivan calculated as he polished his claws.

"A boy?" Arthur chirped.

"A girl," Pepe sighed.

"Someone to restore balance," Kuan Yin continued.

"We'll just have to wait," Ivan said calmly. "Let nature take its course."

Meanwhile, back in the privacy of her atrium suite, Joslin dumped out the contents of her mother's satchel on the bed. She recognized many of the botanicals that her mother used for childbirth. For a brief moment, she wondered about the possibility of delivering a child. Then she rushed outside to a meadow on the other side of the mountain where she could reacquaint herself with her mother's favorite flowers and herbs. Her heart pounded as she raced outside toward the tall grasses on the steppes.

When she reached the meadow, she noticed a hummingbird diving over an array of fragrant wildflowers. She followed the small bird and saw Yuri reclining on the ground. He was thoughtfully looking over the view, which captivated him with its wildlife. Joslin stopped in her tracks. For a brief moment, she wasn't sure whether to approach him. She could not determine whether he wanted to be alone or whether she wanted to be alone with her memories pertaining to her mother's satchel. She turned a half step away and watched the hummingbird dive thirstily into the middle of a small wildflower.

Without looking up or moving, Yuri asked her, "How is the queen today?"

Then he stretched and yawned almost seductively at her. Joslin froze and turned around with the satchel gripped tightly in her hands. The carefree movement of his body disarmed her. She walked toward him and sat down beside him as he stretched a little more. She watched the taut sinews of his muscles expand and contract. Then she placed the satchel down on the ground next to her with a sigh.

"Fine," she answered. "How is Yuri?"

"Yuri is great," he said, moving himself closer to Joslin. "It's a beautiful day and I am alone on a beautiful meadow with a beautiful woman."

Joslin chuckled softly when she heard his words. His hand reached to move back the hair that a soft wind had blown across her face. Then he gazed into her eyes.

She blushed slightly and pulled away. "You are wearing a tiger's eye around your neck."

"Yes," he said. He turned his head to the meadow while gently placing his hand on top of hers.

Several moments of silence passed between them. A light breeze rose through the meadow, swirling the flower heads around them. Joslin accepted the shift in the whisper of the wind and turned towards Yuri.

"I miss my mother. I miss my father," she told him.

"So do I," Yuri delicately agreed. He plucked a blade of straw grass and put one end in his mouth. He handed another to Joslin. She put the stick of grass in her mouth and cautiously savored it.

"I don't want to repeat their history," she confessed, staring towards the horizon. "I want to live to see the children of my children."

"We have a lot to live for," Yuri commented and then added with a hint of a blush, "and we have a lot to create."

Joslin took a deep breath and looked at Yuri again. "I see that you understand my mission."

"It is not just yours," he told her. "I place my stake in the future too."

"I see," Joslin nodded, "that it is more than just something Ivan put in your morning herbed tea."

Yuri rolled back and heartily laughed. "It's my father's legacy as a descendant of the Neanderthals. When they came to this planet, they were on a mission. Ivan helps me survive to see the next day."

Joslin stared into space over the meadow and smiled brightly. Yuri lightly rubbed her shoulder. She took a deep breath and relaxed under his touch. Then he slowly moved toward her, closer and closer until he could see directly into her eyes. Joslin blinked.

"I have a lot to lose, you know," she told him as she studied his eyes.

"We all do," he assured her.

Chapter Twenty-Six

There has got to be

Some basis in reality

For a belief

That frees the soul

Tune Reference: *I Believe I Can Fly*

----R. Kelly

LATER THAT EVENING Joslin met her brother and friends in the reception area. The elves and gnomes from MidEarth had been busy constructing the new meeting room, complete with several kitchenettes and dining space.

"This place is beginning to remind me of the North Pole," Eegan commented when he saw the gingerbread decor in the kitchenettes.

"When you start cooking, you can decide on the decor," Joslin diplomatically told him.

Eegan grinned at the gauntlet that Joslin had thrown at him. Pepe nudged his partner's side and pointed to the tropical flora close to the hot springs. Merlin shrugged and peered at the nearby dining area, which offered a wonderful view overlooking the tropical scene as well as the starlit sky above.

"I have news about Dadgon," Arthur began as he took a mug of steaming mead from the tray that several fairies carried around the reception area.

Joslin turned and faced her brother. She examined his expressionless face for emotional portents, but she found none. Taking a deep breath, she encouraged him to continue.

"He fled the Druid Isle. He went alone without any Sea Dragons. Nobody knows where he went. His sister doesn't know either."

"Is Miriah maintaining her surveillance on the well?"

"Yes, no change there, at least that we can detect," Merlin added.

"Has anyone found the traitors who pursued Nessie?" Joslin asked.

"Yes, they were former friends of Dadgon," Arthur continued.

"Who is running the Druid Isle in Dadgon's absence?" Joslin quizzed.

"I am," Arthur replied. "Dadgon abdicated."

"I am building a castle near my rebirth cave near Yorkshire," Merlin announced. "I think that I'll call it Richmond."

"I'll come and visit," Arthur promised.

"Me too," Joslin added. "The next time that I visit our Saxon cousins, I'll stop by. I want to ask their help in looking for Dadgon. Do you know whether they are aware of the traitors?"

"No, we both have been busy. Constantinople still thinks that I am the Pendragon's son."

"I bet that comes in handy," Joslin quipped.

"Yes, especially when we throw a party," Arthur said dryly.

"Let me guess, armies of little Arthurs are showing up unexpectedly in the populace," Joslin rejoined.

"Oh, they are expected all right," Arthur retorted.

"Anyone special?" asked his sister, getting right to the point.

"Many who claim," he acknowledged. "I really am too young myself. The customs of the previous Pendragon administration don't suit me, but I am too busy fighting for my life to change it yet."

"Hang on," Joslin said. "Just as long as the church doesn't push for you to marry, you should be fine."

Arthur sighed and glanced at the construction going on around him. "I like the switch to iron, myself."

"Seems to hold better than bronze," Joslin remarked.

"So when do I become Uncle Arthur?" her brother asked pointedly.

"I don't know," she said truthfully. "Sometimes I think that the Sea Dragons have more to say about it than my lover or myself. Come by the atrium suite tomorrow for dinner and meet Yuri."

"Where's Yuri now?" Eegan asked.

"He and Ivan are working on a project at the forge," Joslin answered. "I think that he is making a reproduction of one the Santas' flying sleighs."

"Who were the Santas?" Arthur questioned.

"Those were the people who rescued the Arctos' children, including Merilyn's predecessor," Joslin explained. "They were relatives of the gnomes and elves. The survivors became known as the Scythians, who later intermarried with the Neanderthals. Yuri's grandmother was Scythian."

Then Joslin turned to Merlin, who watched the view above them from the ledge outside the meeting area. "When the Dragon flyers arrive from MidEarth, we will begin exploring the cave for a passageway to saltwater. This will enable us to contact the merpeople from our protected position."

"I'll see what they can find on their end," Merlin said. "I'm sure that we will figure out something. I think that there are some saltwater lakes nearby, and that would be a wonderful place to start."

"Also, it would be great to get Dadgon's official word on his abdication so that we know what we are up against," Joslin told him. "I am surprised that he didn't even tell his sister."

Merlin added, "If he doesn't show soon, he will miss out on these utopic events."

Joslin quietly nodded.

"You are not just building a city here," Merlin comforted her. "You are not just adding to the planetary grid. You are also adding to the human consciousness."

"Yes, it's those Sea Dragons again," Joslin wistfully replied. "It's another survival skill wrought by challenging times. It is rough outside of the bubble. We all need a place to go, even if it is inside our own minds. Every mind should be able to track and hold onto this base. Call it the twenty-second dimension. This is it."

"It is like history repeating itself," Merlin murmured. "Instead of the Arctos being physically airlifted to safety from the Serpentines, spiritual people will be lifted here. Instead of ascension, people will transcend."

"My father called it the Inverse. It is the technique when you undo a wrong, neutralize the effect, and take it to higher, healing level," Joslin softly said.

"You are creating a spiritual net for those walking a tightrope," Merlin whispered.

"Outside the bubble, that is the only place for the spiritual to walk," Joslin said in a hushed voice. "I entertain no delusions about reality here, despite the bubble. As you know, we all begin in a nest or womb or even a cocoon. Sometimes, when the going gets rough, we need to be able to go back there in our mind so that we can remember what is like to have no needs."

"Have mercy!" Merlin whistled.

"It is about time we do," Joslin answered before she left the group to retrieve an important message from the crystal in the radio room. As she passed through the opening into the corridor, she called to Merlin, "Don't forget to smell the wildflowers."

"What wildflowers?" Merlin answered, glancing around the room.

"The ones in the meadow on the other side of the mountains," a blue fairy added as she offered the wizard a piping-hot cup of licorice tea.

"Hmm, this is great," he told the fairy while he stared into her deep, blue eyes through the steam from his cup.

She fluttered her wings and sparkled brightly.

"Can you show me around?" he asked her.

Without a word she smiled and with another sparkle motioned for him to follow her.

Meanwhile, Joslin entered the communications room and peered into the crystal at its end.

"What is going on Kuan Yin?" she asked when the image of the goddess appeared.

"The caravan from MidEarth was ambushed after they left the Silk Road for the Altai Mountains," Kuan Yin told her. "One of the Dragon flyers was killed."

"Are they safe now?"

"They made camp just inside the bubble," she answered. "I am still needed on the Silk Road. The MidEarth caravan needs help and supplies. Morale is very low."

A tear escaped Joslin's eye. "Yes. I'll fly out immediately with two of the new flyers."

When Joslin landed near the camp, several flyers from MidEarth came to meet her. She gave them quick hugs and then tossed some small, hard cakes in their direction. They caught them with a weak smile of relief.

"How are the Sea Dragons holding up?"

"After they cleaned up the remains of the ambush, they went foraging," answered McDonnell, who had healed his facial deformity years ago and grown into a handsome young man.

Grabbing a parcel of supplies, Joslin turned and spotted the frozen body of the dead Dragon flyer lying outside the tents. "I see they missed one."

"She asked us to tattoo her body with her drawings and bury her in the frozen mountains for posterity," Donovan replied, producing the artwork from a pocket in her green cloak. Like some of the other caretakers, she had healed and gone on to become a Dragon flyer.

"Now there's a thought," Joslin responded. She pondered the notion of using a dead body as a piece of papyrus and leaving it for someone else to find in the icy mountains. Her musings were quickly interrupted by the words of another caretaker.

"Do you know what it is like hiding a meal from hungry, hard-working Sea Dragons?" Ellis asked rhetorically. Over time he had learned to hear and loved eavesdropping.

Recalling her training exercises surrounded by a pack of ferocious Sea Dragons, Joslin shuddered slightly and replied, " I can imagine."

Chapter Twenty-Seven

Vitality makes a wave

With a huge splash

Tune Reference: *Splish Splash*

----Bobby Darin

"PLEASE HAND ME a towel from the other room!" Joslin shouted as she bathed a small boy. Her clothes were soaked, but she dared not release her grip on the infant. When Yuri came to the door, she explained quietly, "Gerwyn really likes the water. I think that he has my webbed feet."

Yuri strategically maneuvered through the room and handed a soft cloth to Joslin while avoiding the puddles from Gerwyn's hearty splashing. He lightly kissed Joslin on the cheek before ducking behind her for cover. Joslin kept her eye on the small babe.

"That's what happens when you are birthed in the water," Yuri remarked.

Joslin had taken advantage of the warm springs during the delivery. Gerwyn floated to the surface with arms outstretched, greeting the world. He had tried to nurse immediately before Yuri had even cut the umbilical cord.

"He has your eyes," Joslin added. "Nobody will be able to get anything past him, not even his parents. He'll see right through us."

"Nothing like having your own reflection staring back at you," Yuri chuckled. "Do you think he could outstare Ivan?"

Joslin wrapped the infant in the fresh cloth and handed him to Yuri. Yuri lifted the swaddled infant in the air with a little dance. "Stare into the eyes of the tiger Dragon! Wheeee! Let him know who is in charge. Wheeee!"

Joslin laughed at the sight of her lover and son prancing around the room. Gerwyn repeated in a soft coo, "Wheeee!"

"Maybe after Gerwyn learns to sit up," Joslin said.

"Fly in the air," Yuri countered as a joyful taunt.

"After he learns to walk," Joslin continued.

"You know, he smells like you now. He is as fresh as a wildflower on the meadow," Yuri commented as he sailed his son through the air.

The small child happily cooed and rubbed his chubby fingers together in delight. His mother slightly blushed and looked at the wet floor. Raising her head with a shake, she told Yuri with a wry grin, "OK, I'm off to meet with the graduating class of caretakers."

She quickly changed her wet tunic and donned her camouflage armor. Yuri and Gerwyn continued their play while Joslin prepared, taking care not to interrupt them. She stopped for a few moments before leaving the room and sighed. She felt pulled to join them, yet her concerns as queen called to her. Then she realized that she had slipped into a world that she had known long ago as a happy child of two wonderful parents. For a moment she felt a sense of peace and contentment as her loss transformed into a sense of hope and relief. Then she understood the gratitude on the faces of the Dragon flyers at the camp. They had embraced life in the new cave with a sense of wonder and enthusiasm unlike any she had witnesses at the abandoned sea cave. The dance between father and son filled the room with this reflection of new life and light. Smiling to herself, Joslin allowed a burgeoning sense of accomplishment to surface. They had come a long way and she knew that her parents would be proud, just as she experienced this moment in its timelessness. She lingered in her blessed position, appreciating what she had.

"You must kiss the queen good-bye," Yuri announced to his small prince. He carried the baby to his mother, who affectionately welcomed them with a hurried shower of hugs and kisses. "See her off," Yuri said, drawing the infant away and softly cradling him upright in his arms.

Gerwyn responded with one of his all-knowing, contented smiles as Yuri patted his round belly. He seemed to understand his mother's role as regal caretaker of the universe. Somehow he knew that his needs would always be met and conveyed no sense of loss at her departure.

"Come, my Buddha baby," Yuri cooed gently to his son. Then he promised, "We have work to do too. I'll bring you to Mama when you are ready for your third breakfast."

Joslin beamed at Yuri, grateful for his assistance. She turned on her heels and left. Walking a few steps down the corridor, she overheard a few grumbles from Gerwyn. She slowed until they quickly passed and Yuri comforted him. Moving a fallen tear from her cheek, she went on her way.

Elissa met her in the hall at the end of the corridor. "Skip class and come for a ride. You haven't flown since the pregnancy and there is something you need to see."

"I was doing you a favor, especially during the first trimester," Joslin retorted dryly. "Sea Dragons don't come equipped with vomit bags."

Everything that Joslin's mother had taught her about caring for pregnant women came back to her. She understood the second reason why her mother had given up Dragon flying, especially the last year of her life, which marked the beginning of her brother's.

Elissa flashed her sparkly Sea Dragon eyes at her and Joslin relented. "OK, I'll keep it short and get Merlin to take over." Noticing the look of concern on the face of the golden Sea Dragon queen, Joslin asked, "What is it that I need to see?"

"The light of day, a real one, not just a reflected or a crystalized one," Elissa answered with a puff of steam for emphasis.

Joslin watched the puff of smoke disappear in the artificial, though spectacular light of the cave. She knew that she could not refuse the Sea Dragon. After making a brief but solid presentation to the class of graduating Dragon flyers, she left Merlin to his own magic and met Elissa, who was waiting for her outside the original entrance of the cave. She quietly climbed aboard, feeling a few pounds lighter than half a year ago. The mighty, golden Sea Dragon spread her wings and soared to the heights over the Altai Mountains. The snow of the mountains glistened in the sunlight below them. A sense of peace had settled over the area, warming the rough terrain with the air of everlasting continuity.

"When are you and Yuri getting married?" the golden Sea Dragon queen quizzed. She softly winked at Joslin.

Joslin sighed, "I knew that you were going to ask me that."

"Well..." Elissa pressed.

"After the baby is walking and talking," Joslin stated emphatically, taking care not to overindulge the Sea Dragon queen. "I wanted him to know what he was getting into...and be able to speak for himself."

"Oh, so he did pop the question," the all-knowing Sea Dragon surmised.

"So?" Joslin replied, shaking her head as if to shake the Sea Dragon off her track.

"You put him off?" the Sea Dragon queen speculated.

"Only a year and a half," Joslin admitted. "I wanted to get through the pregnancy."

"And then some…" Elissa said, landing on a steppe on the other side of the mountains.

Joslin dismounted quickly and looked at the frozen ground that would erupt with wildflowers next spring. "They killed Wayne and Minerva and destroyed the village. I am healthy, but the grief almost cost me the pregnancy. I can't take anymore."

"I heard from the others," Elissa said warmly. "You were very busy and maintained your role well under pressure. I am glad you kept your baby."

Joslin sobbed and nodded. "I hate feeling fragile."

Elissa softly planted a light kiss on her cheek. She added with a smirk, "It keeps you in touch with the fragility of the baby. Gerwyn is fine with it."

Joslin wrapped herself under one of the great wings of the golden Sea Dragon queen and wept. "I almost feel guilty about the utopia that we have created here. I will miss Wayne and Minerva so much."

"We all will miss their play and wisdom," Elissa comforted Joslin. "They wanted you to continue with your life. Whether you realize it or not, the baby brings us all hope. They heard that you were pregnant. You do not know how much that brightened their hearts and souls. They almost escaped with that knowledge, but their opposition was too strong. We are all left to our lives and missions, not someone else's. They, of all people, understood and accepted that. They were great guardians for you and your brother."

Joslin quieted and dried her eyes.

"As soon as Arthur heard that you were officially active again, he began his journey," Elissa told her. "I expect him to appear in a portal any minute now."

Joslin grinned. She could remember finding him as a wandering toddler in the Pendragon's tent. Now he was looking forward to his new role as uncle.

"He can't keep up with all his children," Joslin chuckled.

"That is probably best, given the historical evidence," Elissa said pointedly. "Your parents' enemies will never be able to track them all either. You are an aunt to most of the British Isles."

Joslin took a deep breath and shrugged. "Let's see if we can find Gerwyn's uncle."

Chapter Twenty-Eight

Parenting gives

Children hope

Tune Reference: *I Hope*

----Dixie Chicks

A FEW MONTHS after Arthur's visit, Joslin journeyed to Wales where she had spent her childhood underneath Wayne and Minerva's guardianship. Rather than return to the site of their cottage, she met the Celtic bishop in the town of Menvera. Patrick, the bishop, had been a close friend of the Green Knights of Camelon and had known her guardians very well. She had learned that Patrick was dying and wanted to see him before he passed.

"I am sorry about Wayne and Minerva," Patrick said in greeting as he embraced Joslin. Then he added, "The Roman Empire has had an influence here as well. They have taken over the diocese and reorganized them into monasteries like they did in Briton."

"Arthur says that we still have a foothold here," Joslin replied.

"That's why I sent for you," continued the wizened bishop, who was beginning to remind her of a druid wizard. "I had a premonition of a rebirth for Wales, and we'd like your blessing."

Joslin almost read his mind. "It involves the niece of Wayne and Minerva, doesn't it?"

"Yes, Non, the daughter of Lord Cynyr of Caer Goch escaped Ceredigion. She now lives with your Saxon cousins in Northumbria. She left Dewi, her child, in our monastic care. It would have been another captured child for the Serpentines, but the Thunder People intervened during the birth. They were unable to reach mother and child during the lightning storm. King Ceredig considers the child as his own, though Non became the life partner of your brother Arthur. They had a covert relationship. The Ceredigion kingdom intends to raise an army of Sants for the Holy Roman Empire. King Ceredig calls himself Sanctus Rex Ceredigionis." Patrick paused briefly before staring at Joslin and resuming, "Dewi has your blue eyes, whereas brown is the color of Non's and Ceredig's eyes."

"Does Arthur know about his son?" Joslin asked, perplexed about the cyclic turn of events. "Ceredig is a distant relative of ours as well as Constantin. Hen Cole otherwise known as Colius II of Colchester placed his bet on Constantinople, whereas my great-grandfather, King Cole, remained with the natives. Hen Cole is his Welsh name. The Serpentines could influence his side of the family with their breeding."

"We have the consent of both parents to raise their son in the monastic tradition of the saintly druids," Patrick replied. The Dragon flyers of Wales must go underground."

"Underneath the noses of the Roman Empire," Joslin commented.

"The Dragon flyers will be invisible to them," Patrick promised. "They are blinded by their own lust for wealth and power. Aesthetics do not concern them."

"Thank you for your wisdom, Patrick," Joslin answered. "They can travel through portals to our base in the Altai Mountains when it is appropriate."

Then she left before anyone noticed Elissa waiting in the forest around town.

After spending a year settling the European Dragon flyers through the portals to Altai, Joslin wedded Yuri in an enormous international ceremony on the meadow with the wildflowers. Dragon flyers from all around the world came to celebrate the occasion. Many knew that it also signaled a new addition to the Stonehenge network. The wedding connected the utopia created in the Altai Mountains to the collective consciousness. The ceremonial ritual marked the completion of the spiritual safety net that Merlin had recognized years earlier.

"Mom, I like your eye shadow," Gerwyn said to his mother as she prepared for the ceremony. "It makes your eyes look bigger."

Joslin glanced into the mirror again and studied the minute fish scales that had suddenly appeared around her eyes for beauty enhancement. She noticed that they did seem to highlight her best features, which were her blue eyes and high cheekbones. Then she turned her attention to Gerwyn and straightened his white tunic.

"Thanks, Gerwyn. I think the new scales are here to stay," she said as she smiled at the young boy. "Time for you to go find Daddy. He is going to need his best man."

Gerwyn beamed and stood erect as his mother applied the finishing touches to his dress.

"Gerwyn!" his father roared from outside the tent. "Where is my best man?"

Gerwyn proudly hurried out of the tent. Joslin rose and faced Kuan Yin, who radiated beside her. The goddess not only was giving away the bride, but she was serving as matron of honor. "I think that we are ready to begin."

Kuan Yin smiled and peered outside the tent. She gave the signal for the procession to begin. First came the Sea Dragons led by their golden queen, Elissa, who was escorted by Earl. They paraded through the meadow in order of cocooning with the Russian Sea Dragons at the back of the line. Next came their caretakers, then the Dragon flyers. Yuri ended the procession and remained at the altar in the heart of the meadow. Eegan and his intergalactic friend, Imaile, officiated. The Three Wise Men stood behind them underneath the cloudless summer sky. Merlin and Arthur sat in the meadow in front of the altar on the bride's side. Several tribes of Scythians and Yeti sat on the opposite side in front of the altar.

Kuan Yin accompanied Joslin down the path to the heart of the meadow where Yuri and the others stood. Then she stopped and stood beside Merlin before Joslin joined Yuri's side. Gerwyn sat in the lap of one of the Yeti and watched his parents. Monarchs of many nations and clergymen of different traditions were seated behind the families of the bride and groom. Fairies, gnomes, and dwarves dotted the countryside along with warriors from many countries and folks. Representatives from several nations brought treaties to the altar to be signed by the queen bride. They were treaties of peace and prosperity. Afterwards, King Ormuz presented Joslin with a solid diamond scepter that had been created by the African Sea Dragons.

"This symbolizes the new rulership outside of the compromises made for the Garden of Eden," the king announced. "No more compromise."

In the tradition of Joslin's father, King Arcas, both Fitzgerald and O'Kennedy presented a coat of arms for the knights of the utopic kingdom. These were the Dragon flyers who had carried on for the fallen flyers, the ones from the families of the crucified Green Knights. The Serpentines had purposely crucified the Green Knights in a particular manner to annihilate their spiritual connection to the planet. The safety net created by the ceremony would offer spiritual protection for the earth spirits and knights that died protecting it. They rode on the back of a white unicorn through the meadow. The white unicorn had a crystal spiral above its third eye. It radiated powerful streams of rainbow light in the sunny meadow. The Dragon flyers handed the banner illustrating the coat of arms to Joslin. The background of the crest consisted of a black-and-white chessboard. On the chessboard was a picture of the white unicorn with the crystal spiral. Through the Armageddon fought by King Arcas, they won their innocence back. The game was over in the minds of those gathered in the utopic kingdom.

Dadgon brought the last symbol piece to the couple at the altar. He solemnly carried a violet, velvet cushion with the crown of thorns. The congregation in the meadow gasped as he placed the relic on the table near Joslin. The bride looked at Dadgon, who bowed his head slightly before quickly leaving to sit beside King Arthur, his half-brother.

"It is from the merpeople," Eegan explained to those who had gathered. "King Arcas' friend, the Lady of the Lake, gave it to Dadgon to place on the altar, signaling the end of the thorns in life."

"Greek brides would wear thorny crowns at their wedding to remind the grooms to be patient with them," Imaile added. "Yuri has been a very patient groom."

Joslin blushed slightly but offered no further explanation. She merely gave Yuri a single nod as if to say, "Let's get on with it." Followed by, "You don't know half of it."

Yuri grinned uncomfortably under the circumstances and began to state his vow to Joslin, "Do you, Joslin, take my hand…"

After he had finished and obtained her consent, Joslin said her vow: "Do you, Yuri, take my hand …"

Eegan introduced the couple as "husband and wife" before Imaile interjected, "You may now seal the deal."

With the final word from Imaile, Yuri and Joslin kissed each other in the meadow as they had done almost three years earlier. Then Yuri lifted his bride onto the white unicorn with the crystal spiral. Yuri collected Gerwyn from the arms of the Yeti grandfather, who brought the small boy to the altar. He placed the boy in front of Joslin before mounting the white unicorn himself. Together they rode off into the sunset and lived happily ever after.